DATE DUE

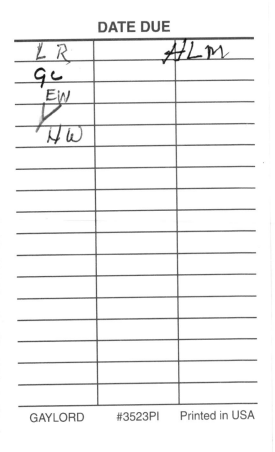

L R,		ALM
GC		
EW		
HW		

GAYLORD   #3523PI   Printed in USA

MORGAN VALLEY

**Center Point
Large Print**

**This Large Print Book carries the
Seal of Approval of N.A.V.H.**

MORGAN VALLEY

LAURAN PAINE

CENTER POINT PUBLISHING
THORNDIKE, MAINE

This Center Point Large Print edition
is published in the year 2008 by arrangement with
Golden West Literary Agency.

The text of this Large Print edition is unabridged. In other
aspects, this book may vary from the original edition.
Printed in the United States of America.
Set in 16-point Times New Roman type.

ISBN: 978-1-60285-093-4

Cataloging-in-Publication data is available from the Library of Congress.

Contents

ONE
The Brothers-in-law

Clifford Stanton drew upon more than twenty years as a stage driver when he finished studying the roadway and said, "It's not a Greenwood rig, Sam, and if I was to guess I'd say it was one of those mud-wagons from up around Raton. You see how wide them rear tires are?"

The other graying, sun-browned, sinewy man stepped forward and chewed a moment staring earthward. He spat amber, straightened back and gazed southward down across the sun-splashed nearly flat countryside.

Cliff Stanton did not turn. He had already looked down there without seeing a stagecoach. He paced slowly northward beside the wheel marks, lips pursed, dead-level gray eyes bright with hard interest, and when the lawman called he turned with a faint frown.

Sam said, "Let's get on back."

Cliff twisted to slowly rake the northward roadway up as far as the green pass with its pine-stands on both sides of the slot, hung there briefly, then with quickened step hiked ahead a dozen yards, stooped to pick up something, and stood so long at this place that Sheriff Hart walked up wearing an interested look.

Cliff handed over two-thirds of a worn horseshoe without saying a word as he continued to study the ground.

For the sheriff a worn-thin shoe which had been cast upon a public road did not mean the thing had come from one of the horses pulling that stage, but he turned it over and studied it closely before saying as much.

Cliff rolled a smoke and lit it before moving closer then pointing to the overlay. "Then it came off the horse that came right along directly behind the coach, because you can see for yourself, Sam, that's the most recent set of tracks. And look there—another set right behind and to the left of that set. So if he was riding down right behind the coach, he was leading a second horse." Cliff turned a sardonic look upon his companion. "And about those other fresh tracks to the left and parallel and—"

"All right," exclaimed Sam Hart, "all right. It was a mud-wagon and this shoe come off one of its horses. Now let's get on back. I got to make up a posse."

Cliff sauntered beside the lawman back where their horses stood hipshot in meager tree shade, untied, turned his animal once then swung up across leather. He smashed out the smoke atop his saddlehorn and gazed at his friend with grave eyes.

"You're not going to catch up, Sam," he announced. "I don't care what them folks told you, that there stage didn't pass southward any couple of hours ago."

Sheriff Hart reined up onto the road-bed before saying, "What the hell are you talking about; that lady and her husband was *on* that stage. They walked from up here on down to town. After they was robbed and set afoot. If anyone knows what happened and *when* it happened it's got to be them folks."

Cliff Stanton sighed, said no more for a while, and enjoyed the springtime sun across his shoulders and down his back. A man wasn't old at forty-five unless he thought of himself as being that way. Cliff's wife of seventeen years had died last autumn. He had become old beginning the day she went into the ground out back of town, and he still was old even though some interest in life was just now beginning to show again.

He and Sam Hart had been friends for many years. Longer even than Cliff Stanton had been married to Elizabeth Hart, the sheriff's sister. They were very much alike in many ways; each had been formed and sustained on the frontier, had the convictions and principles of frontiersmen. They were not talkative men, they were shrewd and experienced and knowledgeable about their world and their environment, and they had seen much change over the past couple of decades. Another time, they might have suspected Indians had raided that coach, except that if that had happened neither that man nor his wife would have arrived on foot back in town, alive.

Cliff had rooftops in sight when he said, "It's just not right, somehow, Sam."

Hart turned. "What's not right?"

"Why would they set those folks on foot no more'n three miles from town after robbing them?"

"Outlaws aren't smart, Clifford, or they wouldn't be outlaws."

Cliff turned a pained expression upon the sheriff. They rode closer to town, could in fact see the full

9

length of Main Street where it ran arrow-straight from the north to the south, before Cliff also said, "Outlaws don't have to be smart, but my guess is that these particular ones are a long way from being dumb."

Sheriff Hart used Cliff's earlier remark against him when he said, "Then why *did* they set those folks on foot where they could walk on down into town?"

Cliff had no answer. "I'll be darned if I know. Did they put up at the rooming-house?"

"That's where I sent 'em."

Nothing more was said. They rode down through and stabled their horses with Saul Hanson at the liverybarn, returned together to the sun-bright roadway and as the sheriff turned aside to jettison surplus tobacco juice, the former stager glanced up in the direction of the only rooming-house in Centreville—in all Morgan Valley for that matter. The sheriff grunted, walked past heading for his jailhouse office leaving Cliff Stanton still standing there, sunk-set gray eyes veiled by thought.

It was one of those bell-clear days. A man could even see a tree-fringe atop the northward mountains, which curved around Morgan Valley to the east and west. The sky was pale turquoise in color. The mountains were dark, as they always were, and the gently rolling range-land between Centreville and the flinty little lower-down foothills, stood between pale green and forest-shadowed dusky brown.

Southward, Morgan Valley ran for a hundred miles before being stopped short against more mountains, the

Amarillos, a corruption of their proper Spanish name, *Amarillez,* meaning yellow, although even the corruption was unknowingly another way of saying the same thing in Spanish.

Once, all this territory had belonged to Mexico. It was still largely inhabited by "Messicans", but they had long since lost any hold they might ever have had, but their customs still predominated in many ways.

The man who came over from in front of the general store to greet Cliff Stanton was a Mexican, an older man, older in fact than Cliff, and whose features were darkly firm and pleasant. He had been badly injured riding for the Morgan family several years earlier and although the limp was almost gone now, he still suffered from hip and back pains now and then. No one riding full-tilt to head cattle when his horse went down, recovered quickly, and if they had been over fifty when that happened there was an excellent chance they might never really recover, not even when they were as lean and fit as Alfonso Gutierrez had been.

He stood a moment regarding Stanton, then said, "That time you got sick at the saloon? That's how you look right now."

Cliff turned and smiled a little. "Got a problem, Al." He considered the ageless, smooth dark face of his friend. "Some folks was robbed on a mud-wagon north of town last night—well, early this morning—and set on foot. They walked to town and told Sam about it."

Gutierrez saw nothing remarkable about this. He shrugged. "It happens."

"Maybe. But if I was goin' to rob folks I wouldn't set 'em afoot where they could just about see any rooftops. Would you?"

Gutierrez had to turn that over several times in his mind. He stared at the dust, shifted his weight to the other leg, then raised his eyes. "All right," he said in his nearly accentless English, the product of his formative years having been spent in a mission school for orphans. "It don't make good sense."

"Yeah, that's what I told Sam," Stanton dryly said.

Gutierrez then offered about the same thought the lawman had offered. "But maybe they didn't know town was down here, or maybe they was dumb enough to do something like that."

Cliff gave Alfonso Gutierrez the same pained look he had given his brother-in-law, but he had no answer for that.

Gutierrez looked up the drowsy roadway with its share of people along both sides on the plankwalks, with a buggy and four or five horsemen moving out in the wide, dusty roadway of late springtime.

"Where did the coach go, afterwards?" he asked.

Cliff jerked his head. "Southward—with one horse wearing only three shoes, and them worn down. And it wasn't one of the Greenwood rigs. It wasn't even a stage it was a mud-wagon."

Gutierrez brushed that aside in one sentence. "There's darned little difference. If it wasn't one of the local rigs, whose was it?"

Cliff had no answer to that either. "I don't know. Sam

and I rode back to look at the sign. We found where they'd put those folks off. That's all."

Alfonso lifted an old hat to lightly scratch his jet-black hair shot through with gray, then resettled the hat. "What's worryin' you is that someone slipped up, and did something dumb. Cliff, the world is full of them, and they're doing dumb things every day." Gutierrez's glance slid to the front of the saloon. "There's a fresh batch of *cerbeza* at the saloon," he murmured hopefully, "and it's hot standing out here."

Cliff too gazed northward to the east side of the roadway. He had not visited Sandal's bar more than two or three times since last autumn, had felt no desire to drink in that length of time, had in fact felt little desire to do any of the things he had once done when his wife had been alive, and Gutierrez knew this as did everyone else around Centreville.

"I'll buy," Alfonso said, as added inducement. They were old friends. A recuperating cowboy without funds could always find an extra silver coin deep down to help an old friend overcome something with a drink of new beer. No man should grieve the rest of his life; the dead, fine though they once were, had gone. Life belonged to the living.

Gutierrez turned to recross the roadway. *"Venga,"* he softly said, "come along."

A pair of faded rangemen were riding past. One nodded at Alfonso and gazed past where Cliff Stanton was standing and said, "There's fat trout in the falls below Red Rock again."

Cliff smiled. He knew all the permanent riders. This particular man was named Jess Turnbow and he worked for the Morgan ranch northeast of town. He was a top-hand, almost a rangeboss and he was just about Cliff's age. They had hunted the mountains together in autumns past, and in summer they had fished the Red Rock pools some Sundays.

"I'll come out some Sunday," he told the rider, and waited until the horsemen were past before following Alfonso across to the far plankwalk, then northward toward Barney Sandal's saloon.

TWO
Sandal's Place

Cliff had not met that man and woman who had been robbed and set afoot, but after Sheriff Hart returned from up north with his brother-in-law, he went up to the rooming-house just before suppertime to talk with them again. It was too late afterwards to make up a posse and go searching for that stage even though vehicles that size usually remained on the road and even though there would be enough of a moon this night to make out wide tire marks.

Sheriff Sam Hart did not rush into things. He had been a lawman long enough to be fairly philosophical about crime and criminals. Moreover, in the back of his mind was a small doubt, a slight degree of skepticism put there by his brother-in-law. While he had been talking to that man and wife at the rooming-house he

14

had also been trying to figure out how, if they had lied to him, they had done it, and more important, *why* they had done it.

He had tried to pin them down about the exact time they had been put off the coach. They told him they had boarded up at Tanque Verde, their destination Preston twenty miles below Centreville. They had relatives there they had been on their way to visit. Their name was Fairchild, the same name as those relatives down at Preston. They had been robbed and put off the stage at about four in the morning. It had taken them from four until about daylight to reach Centreville, walking along with an occasional rest. All they could tell Sam about the men who had robbed them was that they had been inside, also passengers, and had suddenly drawn guns, halted the coach, robbed the passengers—Mr. and Mrs. Fairchild, the only other passengers—had shoved them out and had ordered the driver to go on.

"Four in the morning?" Sam had asked. "You pretty sure of the time?"

The man and woman had exchanged a fleeting look, then the man had said, "I didn't look at my watch because those highwaymen took it off me, but I remember looking at it shortly before they stopped the coach and robbed us. It had to be about four, Sheriff. Maybe a few minutes one way or the other, but close to four o'clock in the morning. Dark as the inside of a well, too."

"What did those men look like?"

Fairchild looked at his wife, a plain woman with

15

severely pulled back dark hair and a thin mouth to match thin, wide eyes. She said, "They didn't look much different from all other rangemen, Sheriff, and they were sitting inside with us so about all I can tell you is that there were two of them, dressed as rangeriders, maybe thirty or forty, without anything I'd remember. They could have been any one of hundreds of hired hands."

That had been no help at all. In fact his entire second interrogation had been of no more help than his first talk with those people had been. But he was not surprised; very few victims remembered much beyond the size of the gun barrel they had looked into.

Sam went back to his office at the jailhouse to blow down the lamp mantle and afterwards lock up for the night, then he went along to the cafe for supper. He was a single man, had never been either married nor even close to it, had a room up there at the rooming-house and ate most of his meals at the cafe northward from his jailhouse on the same side of the roadway.

His life was simple by most standards. Excepting an occasional fight, usually at Sandal's place and usually on a Saturday night, his official duties did not overtax him. The last crime which had occurred in Centreville had been when the blacksmith, Charley Hoffman, had shot and killed a traveling man who had been visiting Charley's wife while Charley was down at his shop sweating. Someone got careless, either the woman or the traveling man, and Charley walked in right after mid-day. The traveling man had died instantly and

Charley's wife went out a bedroom window. She got out of town and Morgan Valley on someone else's saddled horse. The animal had been recovered ten miles below town and the woman, who had probably flagged a ride with freighters, was never seen again.

Charley Hoffman had been acquitted by a jury of townsmen. Even so, he had closed the smithy's doors one Friday, climbed aboard one of the Greenwood Company's northbound stages and no one had heard a word about him afterwards. That had happened almost six years earlier. Since then Sam Hart had broken up some dogfights on Main Street, had located several young runaways, had jailed a few dozen rangemen for being drunk in public, had chased his share of horsethieves—without recovering but one horse, the others having disappeared in the mountains where bands of hold-out ragheads had secret *rancherias*—and had lived his normal existence between the jailhouse, the cafe, and the rooming-house.

Nor did he go out of his way looking for things which would bother him. Now, seated at the cafe counter slowly downing what was called elk stew and which he privately thought might be aged mule, he irritably reconsidered Cliff Stanton's little disquieting comments, and what particularly stuck in his craw was the fact that he too had been convinced, from the condition of those tracks up yonder, that the mud-wagon and those folks which had got off it up there, had stopped at least four hours earlier than the Fairchilds told him they had been put off.

On the other hand, as the man had said, he no longer had his watch. True, they had been victimized and were understandably distraught over that.

Still—if they had been put off at midnight rather than four in the morning, and by their own account they had walked steadily with only occasional pauses to rest, why hadn't they reached town until daybreak?

The cafe man came padding out to scratch an ample girth and gaze at the sheriff's half-full plate. After so many years cafemen got to know the feeding habits of their old customers. He stopped scratching long enough to say, "You don't like the stew, Sam?"

Hart looked down. "Yeah, it's all right, Will."

"You ain't eatin' it."

Sam was already in an irritable mood. "Is there a law says I got to bolt it down?"

The cafeman regarded his customer's bronzed face a moment, then turned without another word and padded back behind his curtained-off cooking area.

Sam left the cafe to stand a moment in the late evening making one of his habitual surveys of the roadway, which was empty except for a few horses here and there at tie-racks.

Over at the general store, which normally would have been dark and locked for the night this late, three men were visible through the roadway window leaning near the proprietor's cluttered little office, talking. One of them was Martin Hamm, owner of the store. Another was Frank Morgan, the biggest and richest cowman in Morgan Valley, grandson of the old trapper who had first visited these parts and who had in his later years not only staked out the ranch holdings but who had also at one time owned most of Centreville.

Sam understood why Martin still had the store open. The Morgan ranch was Martin Hamm's most affluent customer. Martin had said as much to Sam Hart many times. In fact Frank Morgan was without question the most affluent cowman in all Morgan Valley, and well he could be, having had it all handed him after his grandfather and father had got it all built up and paid off before Frank came along to inherit.

Sam knew Frank, had known him for many years, but not as a friend, particularly. The Morgan family only lived part of the year at the ranch; they were wealthy people who traveled a lot and who very often wintered back east where the social environment was better than anywhere in New Mexico Territory, including ancient and courtly Albuquerque.

He felt around for his plug, gnawed off a corner, pouched the cud while watching two rangemen leave Barney Sandal's place to mount up and turn westerly out of town, and decided to have a nightcap. It was Wednesday, things would be quiet for another couple of nights, and he was a little tired from that earlier ride out and back with his brother-in-law.

Cliff was no longer at Barney Sandal's bar but Alfonso Gutierrez was, leaning in pleasant reverie until the sheriff stepped up beside him and said, "Buy you a round, Al," then the *vaquero's* happiness seemed to fade slightly.

"Can't return it," he told Sam Hart.

The sheriff winked at Barney and held up two fingers. Sandal, a short, beefy individual running a lot to flab these last few years, brought two glasses and a bottle of sourmash whisky.

Sam wordlessly filled both glasses, shoved one in front of Gutierrez and said, "It's on the house, but Barney don't know it yet. I don't have any money with me either."

Al laughed, downed his jolt and shuddered behind tightly closed black eyes. When he recovered he looked injuredly at the label on the whisky bottle. "It was never that bad before, Sheriff."

Sam shuddered a little too, and mopped his eyes with a soiled cuff. "It's not the same stuff that came in the bottle, Al. Barney saves the bottles and refills them with his own slosh. And that was pretty bad, wasn't it?"

"Terrible!"

"Want another one?"

"Yeah."

They stood a moment, though, before dropping down the second one. Alfonso said, "Cliff was in here a while back. We had a beer."

Sam nodded his head. "I'm glad he's comin' out of his shell a little. Only it seems to me it's takin' him a long while."

Al raised reproachful dark eyes. "She was your sister."

Sam's attitude had nothing to do with that. "Al; she was all the family I had left. She was nice and pretty and a good cook. I loved my sister. . . . But she's dead. *Comprende?*"

Gutierrez indeed understood. He had tried to say this same thing to Cliff. On the other hand Alfonso was an emotional individual. After one beer and one jolt of green whisky, reaching for the second jolt of whisky, he became even more emotional. As he lifted the glass a suspicion of tears appeared in his eyes. "To your sister, *jefe,* may she have died in His grace."

They downed the jolts almost simultaneously. Afterwards they stood like stones, gripping the bartop with both hands until Barney came along, his pale eyes friendly. "You boys doing all right?"

Alfonso's gaze of reproach was heavily misted by tears. Sam said, "Someday, Barney, someone is going to get mad enough to shoot you. That's the worst gawddamned whisky I ever drank in my whole life."

Sandal was unperturbed. "Wait, Sam. Give it another month to mellow. See how light-colored it is? Well, whisky's no good until it gets sort of amber-dark. That's when it's getting age on it."

"Then why did you put it green into that darned bottle?"

"Sam, I got to have whisky to serve. That's my business. Folks come in here for whisky and beer. I can always make a batch of beer in a week or two, but whisky takes a lot longer, and—"

"You're going to kill somebody with that stuff, some day," murmured Alfonso, hitching up his trousers with one hand and mopping wet eyes with his sleeve on the other hand.

Sandal considered Gutierrez. He did not like Mexicans. He did not forbid them to visit his bar, but he could not hide his dislike even then. "Drink over at the *cantina* behind town," he told Alfonso. "Anyone who'd guzzle *tequila* and *pulque's* got nerve to say my liquor isn't good."

Sandal marched back up where a pair of townsmen were leisurely sipping beer. He did not return and in fact he did not even glance down where the sheriff and the *vaquero* were standing.

The whisky worked, though. Sam saw one and a half faces of himself in the back-bar mirror. He firmly stoppered the bottle and pushed it as far as his left arm would reach, then he said, "Al, how are you feeling?" He meant how rapidly was Gutierrez recovering from his back and hip injury.

The answer he got referred to Alfonso's present condition. "Just about drunk, Sam. It may be poison but it can make a man drunk."

"Naw, Al, not *that*. How's your back and all—how are you feeling *that* way?"

Gutierrez blinked at the pair of solemn brown faces which were blinking back at him from the back-bar mirror. "Better. I went down to Preston and saw the doctor. He said I was doing very well. What does he know, Sam? He didn't even make me take off my shirt, didn't even push with his fingers."

"Sure. Three dollars?"

"Two. Because I'm a poor ignorant greaser. Sometimes it pays to be one. I even removed my hat and held it in front of me."

Sheriff Hart looked disapprovingly down his nose. "That's downright dishonest, Alfonso."

"Well, so is being a doctor, most of the time. Anyway, I didn't have three dollars. I only had two, and I had to borrow them from Saul Hanson."

Sam turned back towards the mirror. There were now two distinct Sam Hart faces looking sweatily back at him. He stared them down as he composed what he wanted to say next.

"Al, I need a man around the jailhouse couple hours a day."

"No," murmured the dark man, but smiled gently. "No, *compadre*. I will get by. Anyway, I don't like the smell of your jailhouse."

"What smell, damn it all!"

"Any Monday morning, Sam, after you have the cells full of those drunk cowboys. Those *borachos*."

Sheriff Hart was an honest man, but now he was torn between the truth and his loyalty to his jailhouse. The truth won. "Yeah, well sometimes they do heave their bootstraps. But I usually fetch in buckets of water and sluice the place out." He did not mention the job again. Later, when they departed from the saloon, both measuring each step, walking with heads up and shoulders squared in the manner of drunks who chose to conceal their true condition, Barney Sandal gazed after them without a trace of goodwill for either of them. Not tonight anyway.

THREE
Curiosity

Cliff went down very early the following morning, got a horse from Hanson's dayman who had just come to work, and rode quietly and slowly out of town, southward.

His brother-in-law had not appeared on the plank-walk yet. In fact although there were a few lights sputtering feebly after having just been lighted, Centreville for the most part was still dark and slumbering.

There were some problems to living alone, as Cliff had discovered. One of them was the lack of any kind of schedule. With a wife, a man who arose early awaited breakfast. He never doubted that she would be there in the evening when he got home, either, so his life slipped into a comfortable and predictable—and deadly—routine. Cliff Stanton had enjoyed every day and month and year of it. He was what every wife wanted her husband to be; a tame animal.

Now she was gone and Cliff's private personality was gradually freeing itself. It had never died, it had simply hibernated.

He was by nature and lifelong habit an early riser. Otherwise he would not be riding southward now when it was still dark and would continue to be that way for another couple of hours.

He was also a thoughtful, quiet man who spoke either in good humor or when he had something to say. He

24

never spoke to be making sounds. He and his brother-in-law were alike in this respect.

Cliff was also a shrewd man. If he hadn't been he never would have survived all those years driving coaches. He had lost count of the number of times he had been halted and threatened with death by highwaymen. He had likewise forgotten the number of brushes he'd had with Apache ragheads, but that had been a long time back; there hadn't been any genuine bronco Indians in northern New Mexico now in quite a while, and Cliff did not miss them. One damned bit. Nor the highwaymen. Nor, for that matter, the rigorous schedules, the blazing heat, the numbing cold, the scourging winds nor even the magnificent spring and summer dawns.

It took time, but he was learning to live alone, to be his natural self, and for a fact he was just now beginning to enjoy the freedom of thought and movement, although this particular morning he was not sure he was doing anything very reasonable. It was so dark, after the moon departed, it was like peering inside a boot, and what Cliff was looking for was wide tire marks.

The reason he was out so early was simple enough. He in fact probably should have done this yesterday when the north-south stage road had even less wheel and horse tracks overlying previous sign, but he was satisfied about one thing: no matter what vehicles or horsemen had passed along since, those mud-wagon wheel-imprints were too distinctive to be duplicated.

They might have been run-over by other marks, but they would still be distinctive enough wherever he found them to be followable. Another couple of days, though, and they would be hard to see, and if any freight outfits came along with their much wider tires, the mud-wagon tracks would be completely obliterated.

Few freighters came this far north, except those with cargo for Centreville, so that was perhaps an unnecessary worry. Still, Cliff preferred not to run the risk, so as he rode slowly along now, rarely even glancing downward in the darkness, he felt he was on the correct trail while he was at the same time making a good start.

By the time sunrise came he was six or seven miles below town. When he looked back he could not even see the sunshine off tin roofs.

The land on all sides, excepting for the roadway itself, was about as it had been for the previous ten or twenty centuries. It had a gentle roll to it and the springtime grass was taller in some places than it was elsewhere but all of it together made the world down here resemble a pale greeny sea frozen in rolling motion. Sounds carried; a pair of red-tailed hawks high overhead dived at one another in a game and their keening cries rode the soft wind down to Cliff with the perfect blending of mobile and immobile nature.

The marks were there. He halted for minutes to study them. This far south only occasional cow-tracks marred them, and the southbound evening stage straddled them so they were clearly recognizable.

Cliff rolled a smoke for breakfast, loosened his old blanket-coat when the sun reached him, finally, then pushed slowly southward.

He did not expect to find that mud-wagon. He simply was curious about it, and not because someone aboard it had committed a robbery but because there was something wrong about the entire affair.

At ten o'clock he encountered a drift of red-backs passing across from east to west. They had the big M mark on their right ribs which Morgan Ranch put on all its cattle, with a much smaller M on the left shoulder of its saddle-stock.

They were good animals. Cliff was no cowman but he knew upgraded beef when he saw it. These were young cows, many with sassy-fat calves at their sides. He halted back a ways so as not to spook them. He was in no hurry anyway. Even so the cattle orry-eyed him and a squat bull with a rear-end on him like a battering ram turned and wagged his horns, not really menacing but going through his bull-motions because he was supposed to. Cliff grinned at him.

The animals wiped out those mud-wagon tracks for five yards, then they emerged again, smooth, unwavering and arrow-straight southward.

The nearest town down here was Preston, about twice the size of Centreville. He was beginning to believe he would cover the entire distance to Preston, which he did not particularly want to do, when the tracks dipped low in a gravelly place where a little sluggish creek ran, and upon the far side the tracks turned off.

He was out where those undulations were greater now. There were a few tree-stands scattered around, and that creek was traceable by the willows growing profusely along both sides of its crooked, meandering course.

A thin call brought Cliff up in the saddle. A horseman pushed out from among the creek-willows and sat gazing roadward. Cliff grunted in mild surprise. It was Al Gutierrez.

Where they met, a quarter mile from the roadbed Cliff thumbed back his hat and sat staring. Alfonso looped reins round the saddlehorn and swung off, smiling. "You're out early," he said.

"I didn't know you were allowed to straddle a horse yet, Alfonso. It's a far walk back if your legs get to acting up." Cliff also swung off.

"That's what I got for my two dollars from that doctor," Gutierrez said, eyeing Cliff thoughtfully. "He said exercise."

"Straddling a horse?"

Alfonso shrugged. "What other kind of exercise is there?" He turned to jut with his jaw. "I watched you coming. For a while I didn't know who it was. I saw what you were doing . . . The tracks leave the road back at the crossing and go out through there on the far side of this creek. Plain as day." Gutierrez turned back. "Why would a passenger stage go out there?"

Cliff looked; visibility was limited by the density of creek-willows so he stepped back aboard his mount and waited a moment, then led the way to the shallows

28

and splashed across. Upon the far side he saw Alfonso's fresh tracks. They were between two clear mud-wagon imprints going northeasterly following the course of the creek-willows.

Al said, "They stayed close. My guess is that they didn't want to be seen. Otherwise, why travel in spongy ground with a wagon?"

There was another reason—a sore-footed horse—but Cliff simply nodded and poked along following the tracks.

He knew this country out here fairly well and to his knowledge there were no habitations within miles of where they were riding. But maybe that was the idea; maybe those stagers or whoever they were did not want to find any other people.

Alfonso made a wide, sweeping gesture with his rein-hand. "They could camp out here anywhere." When Cliff came to where Alfonso's tracks ended, the *vaquero* said, "I had a bad feeling; like they might be watching me somewhere among the willows. So I turned back and that's when I saw you."

Cliff was interested. "How's come you to be down here?"

Alfonso shrugged. "Curious. Last night I got about half drunk at Barney's saloon and couldn't go right to sleep, so I made black coffee to sober up, and it kept me awake. I kept thinking back to what you'd said . . . I saddled my horse an' rode over through here beside the road until daylight come. Then I made for the creek—and there it was, right where they'd left the road." Al paused to gesture around again. "An' I think if we don't get careful we're going to ride into something."

He was correct, they did ride into something. Because Cliff was out front he saw it first. He halted, let Alfonso come up beside him, and pointed with a gloved hand.

It was a battered old mud-wagon leaning disconsolately close to the bend of the creek where willows which were probably supposed to conceal it, because of their paleness, made the dark vehicle stand out more prominently than ever.

The tongue was on the ground. Harness was flung nearby in careless disarray. There was not a single horse in sight and although Cliff got the feeling of loneliness up ahead, he was also mindful of his companion's worry. He rolled another smoke with his reins looped, lit it, and continued to sit in motionless silence while he restudied the onward scene.

Al Gutierrez, who did not use tobacco, let his black gaze roam the countryside in all directions. He clearly was not at ease and although he was armed with a shell-belted six-gun, he seemed less willing to rely upon this than he was to rely upon his instincts. He finally said, "There's no one."

He was right. When they walked their horses on up to within a yard or two and swung down, only a few agitated little brownish birds flew from the close-by willows, scolding and screaming as they fled farther upstream to again disappear into willow-tops.

The mud-wagon had once had a legend in red paint upon its doors but all Cliff could make out now was something like "Mission", or "Missoula", or maybe it was someone's name that began with M then faded down to illegibility.

The vehicle was old, the wide rear tires were worn to thinness, there were dents and scars and peeling paint where perhaps thirty or forty years earlier there had been fresh paint and a proud bearing. Mud-wagons weren't common any more, not since people had begun gravelling roadbeds so that ordinary stages would not sink to their hubs in the rainy season.

It looked like a stagecoach except that it sat higher on the axles and the undercarriage was built with a view towards hard usage in inclement, muddy weather. It was a little smaller, too, than most stagecoaches even though it looked the same size because it was taller, and where stages would accommodate as many as eight passengers inside, this rig would not carry more than six, and even then they would be hip-to-hip and shoulder-to-shoulder.

Cliff had tooled a few of these things, years back. They handled like top-heavy hat-boxes, but in perfectly level country over muddy roadbeds they were dependable although none of them had been built for the comfort of drivers or passengers. Their sole function was to *get there* and they had usually done just exactly that.

Cliff punched out his smoke upon the top of a high rear wheel and tied his horse to the boot-chains before strolling up ahead to study the harness. It too was old.

It was the variety of chain-harness stagers had stopped using long ago. Like the rig, it was built for strength, not to particularly favor the horses which had to wear it.

He shook his head. "It takes me back to when I was a kid," he mused aloud.

Alfonso, who had never been a stager, was not entirely interested in their discovery. He kept peering among the willows and elsewhere, out over the sun-warmed grassland which ran, empty and clean, for as many miles as a man could see, in three directions, and much farther in fact than a man could see. He tugged loose the tie-down thong on his holstered Colt even though there was nothing to be seen, and even the quiet was depthless out here.

"Where are they?" he plaintively asked.

Cliff had already arrived at a conclusion about that, so he pointed. "Rode off on their harness-animals. Yonder."

The tracks were visible where the spongy creekside pale, short grass grew. Cliff stood gazing in the direction of the tracks, then lifted his hat to scratch.

"Crossed the creek up ahead, I'd guess. Let's go see."

He was correct. The horse-tracks paralleled the willows to a wide place, then they pushed on to the north side. Cliff swore with feeling when a willow branch whipped him across the face. Where cattlemen rode in places like this they usually hacked a pathway. No one had ever done that out here. Nor in all probability would they ever do it. This was a part of the range

32

where riders might pass through, occasionally but they would have little reason to do this more than perhaps once or twice a year, when they were cattle-hunting, and even then they would not have to cross the creek to roust out resting, shaded red-backs, all they would have to do was let the cattle see them.

When they broke clear on the opposite bank they halted to study the tracks. In an area of grass-free mud Cliff pointed. "One horse with three shoes and three shod-horses. They're our lads all right. But if the two passengers inside were highwaymen, what in hell are they taking the driver and gunguard along with them for?"

"Didn't want no one to walk back to town," answered Alfonso matter-of-factly.

Cliff looked around. "Yeah? Then why did they turn those other two folks loose to walk to town? Come on."

The tracks led away from the creek almost due northward, and that puzzled both Alfonso and Cliff Stanton. They had half-expected the riders to cling close to the protective creek-willows. Eventually, Al said, "I'll tell you how it looks to me. They got a destination. They know where they're going."

Cliff said nothing for a couple of hundred yards, then he reined to a halt. "Sam'll be out with a posse some-where this morning."

"He said that?"

"No. Not to me anyway, but I haven't seen him since we got back from the north road yesterday. Only I know Sam; he may be slow but he's not dumb. He'll be

33

running someone's tracks by now, and I'd guess he'll do it with three or four possemen."

"Then I hope he cuts across country, otherwise he's going to be everywhere them fellers *has been* and he'll never get up where they *are*."

The sun was still climbing. The pair of riders could see for miles. There was no movement, no riders in sight anywhere. Alfonso sighed. "They must have lit out before dark, maybe, last night. Or damned early this morning." A thought occurred to him. "Hell; they probably was inland from me this morning while I was riding south and they was going north. We passed, maybe."

"You didn't hear anything?"

"No. But if these tracks keep bearing easterly I wouldn't have anyway. We'd have been maybe a mile or two apart."

"Then what are you worrying about, Al?"

Gutierrez regarded his friend thoughtfully. "It's my nature. Didn't you know us greasers worry a lot?"

Cliff grinned. "How come when I call someone that they want to fight, but when you say it about yourself it's all right."

"Same reason you can call yourself a bastard and I can't."

They struck out across the vast emptiness, dwarfed to ant-size by the immensity of the overhead high blue sky and by the sweep of rolling landform they were riding over.

FOUR
Murder!

For Cliff Stanton the mystery only deepened when they were about two miles from Centreville, as a crow would fly, although they were about three miles eastward when they found a dry-camp.

Alfonso was better at reading sign than his companion was; he found the tracks of that horse with only three shoes. Cliff nodded about this. He had never doubted but that they were on the right trail. What he could make no sense of was what this was all about. Why would men drive a stage so far south of town, then hide it and ride back in the general direction of town? And what in the Lord's name were they up to anyway? And if they had wanted all this subsequent behavior to be so secret, why had they booted out that man and his wife last night, so close to town? The doubt that they had known they were that close to Centreville seemed plausible; rooftops would not have been visible in darkness. But there was a fresh worry for Cliff Stanton. It was beginning to appear to him that those outlaws or whatever they were, *had* in fact known where Centreville was. They were certainly returning to its vicinity now, and even last night when they had passed through, it would not have been too late to turn back and pick up the man and wife.

He let Alfonso Gutierrez lead part of the way while he puzzled over the events which increasingly made less and less sense to him. Only when they found the dry-camp did his mind clear itself of the other questions.

Alfonso gestured. "They were here a long time. Maybe a couple of hours." He raised troubled eyes. "Why would they sit out here?"

Cliff had no idea, but it was clear that they *had* lingered.

The camp was east of a low, fat swell of rolling land. It was hidden from view to anyone approaching from the west, but in the darkness what difference would that make? No one would see the men anyway. No one, in fact, would be out here after nightfall. This was part of Morgan Ranch rangeland; only cattle and some loose-stock horses might be around.

But it occurred to Cliff that since the riders had probably chosen this campsite deliberately, they had done so because they probably had meant to remain here when visibility improved. Maybe they had still been over here at daybreak. If so, then there was a remote possibility that someone might have seen them. But it was a very remote chance.

Only when Alfonso strolled along beside the continuing tracks after the strangers had struck their camp, did something fresh intervene, and this time Cliff could make what he thought was a fairly accurate prediction. Alfonso walked back briskly, grunted for Cliff to get astride, and led the way for about three-quarters of a mile. There, under the high hot sun, Cliff saw the tracks of two riders approaching from the west.

"Rendezvous," he muttered. "I'll be damned. They came up here to meet someone."

Alfonso, who had already surmised this much, looked westerly in the direction of town as he said, "Who? How many people are in this thing?"

They turned in the direction of town, finally, deciding it was time to head back anyway, and saying they would return in the morning to follow the fresh track of six riders which seemed to start out in a big encircling way, heading for the distant mountains.

They discussed things. The only two conclusions they agreed about was that those men were not involved in something they wanted others to know about, and they'd had companions in town. It never once occurred to Cliff who the people might have been who had ridden out, in the dark, to meet the stagers. There were too many other strange things to ponder.

They reached town with the slanting late-day sun reddening as it sank close to the dimmest distant low peaks west of Morgan Valley. No one was at the liverybarn when Alfonso waited for Cliff to put up the horse. Then Cliff went over to Alfonso's mud, two-room *jacal* out back of town where most of the Mexicans lived. This had in fact been the original town, but back in those days it had been called *Ciudad Santa Anna,* which was not only too large a mouthful for *Yanqui* settlers, but it had also commemorated a man *Yanquis* despised, Antonio Santa Anna, eight times *Presidente* of Mexico, the conqueror of the Alamo.

Here, Alfonso corralled his horse, forked it some

feed, and led the way inside where he had a pot of *frijoles* on the little iron stove. It took only moments to heat the beans and ladle them into two bowls, then to sit at a rickety old table and eat. Both men had been since last night without food.

They were scarcely speaking as they ate when a liquid-eyed slim Mexican woman of perhaps thirty-seven or forty, came soundlessly to the doorway and peered in where the room, which lacked windows, was gloomy and pleasantly cool.

She seemed ready to flee at sight of Cliff but Alfonso spoke to her in Spanish and she fidgeted. He asked a question which she answered guardedly. Alfonso put down his spoon and arose with an expression of tired resignation. Cliff ignored them both; the beans were very good or he was very hungry.

Within moments Alfonso returned as far as the doorway and stared in at Cliff. "There's been a killing," he said. Cliff's head came up and around. "Who? What did she say?"

"Martin Hamm at the store. He was killed. They found him inside the store this morning."

Cliff put down his spoon and turned fully. "Inside the store this morning?"

"*Si.* The safe was open and nothing was left in it!"

Cliff arose slowly. "Gawddamn," he exclaimed, and started out of the little house. "Come on, Al."

But Gutierrez remained by his *jacal.* "She told me not to go."

"Why not? Come on, damn it."

"Mexicans killed him, Cliff. They found a *huaracha* and a Mex knife where he was lying. She said the *gringos* are talkin' about lynching Mexicans."

For a moment the two men looked at one another from a distance of about fifty feet, then Cliff grunted and turned on his heel. It dawned on him, now, that Hanson's barn which always had someone around day or night, had been totally empty when he had put up the horse over there. At the time he had thought it was odd, but that's all he had thought, because he was glad to be back and he was tired.

The plankwalks were deserted. Tied horses were along a number of racks but there did not seem to be any people around when Cliff emerged from an alleyway onto Main Street. He saw a big brindle dog snuffling along the far side of the roadway opposite Sandal's saloon and that was all, until someone walked solemnly out of Hamm's store. It was Saul Hanson and he heard bootfalls so he turned to face Cliff. Hanson jerked a thumb over his shoulder. "They cleaned out the safe, neat as a whistle."

Cliff said, "Who did? Where's Sam?"

"Sam? He went out early with some fellers from town to scout up a stage or something; that's what someone told us at Barney's place. Who killed Martin? All's I know is that it was Messicans. His family took him home to lay him out."

Hanson's gaze was dispassionate from shock. "Hell; I knew Martin ever since I come here. He never hurt nobody. Folks say they must have got him out of the house last night, marched him down here and made him open the safe. Then they knifed hell out of him. Barney was comin' to work this mornin' and looked through the window and seen Martin lyin' in the doorway to his little office back yonder." Hanson hitched at his trousers. "Those damned Messicans; sneaky, underhanded folks every damned one of them. Knifin' a man like that. In the back, so help me."

Hanson turned to cross the roadway heading southward in the direction of his liverybarn.

Cliff looked in from the store doorway. There were five or six men back there by the office, softly speaking. One turned and saw Cliff and headed for the doorway. It was Barney Sandal, his thick frame erect with fury, his pale, slaty eyes fierce.

"Where's that greaser you was drinkin' with last night, Cliff? That damned Gutierrez who rode for the Morgans?"

"Down at his house. Why?"

"I'll lay you big odds he had a hand in this. If he didn't he darned well knows who did. He likely come back here last night, drunk as a lord and—"

"He didn't do any such a damned thing, Barney."

"No? Well, maybe you'd like to know what I seen before daylight when I went out back of the house this morning? *Him* riding out of town in the dark; sneakin' along east of the road like he was goin' somewhere to bury the money he had taken from the safe—after he knifed Martin to death!"

"Barney, Al Gutierrez was with me from about daylight on, and he didn't have any money or any knife or any—"

"No, because he left the damned knife stickin' in Martin's back. And if he was with you from daylight on—where was he *before* daylight? And how come him to be ridin' a horse when he's been tellin' everyone around town he couldn't sit a horse? I'll tell you why! Because he darned well *could* ride a horse, but he was plannin' this robbery and murder so he made out like he was too crippled up and folks wouldn't suspect him. That's what he done. . . . I favor hangin' the son of a bitch right now, this morning."

Cliff's anger never came swiftly. It did not come that way now, but the longer he stood looking at the hate-distorted face of the thicker and shorter man before him, the more his knowledge of Sandal's dislike of all Mexicans made him see Barney as both unreasonable and dangerous. He finally said, "Al Gutierrez never robbed anyone in his life, let alone killed anyone."

"You always been soft on them greasers," Sandal retorted.

Cliff balled his hands into fists, anger finally making him willing to strike out. "Barney, you better simmer down. When Sam gets back let him handle this."

"Sam too," said the saloonman. "I've seen him steer drunk Messicans over to Mex-town instead of lockin' them for bein' drunk like he'd do anyone else."

Cliff's face whitened. He said nothing but his look remained fixed on the saloonman until Lew Calkins the saddlemaker whose shop was next to the jailhouse, walked out in his stooped way, and said, "Barney, we better not do it. Not yet anyway. Suppose it warn't him?"

Cliff's anger subsided a little. "Wasn't who, Lew?"

"That hurt Messican who rode for the Morgans . . . Gutierrez?"

"You mean—hang him?"

"Yeah, but I figure we'd better hold off until Sam gets back."

Cliff faced the saloonman again. "Don't you try it," he said quietly.

Sandal was in no mood to listen or to compromise. "Why? You think you could stop ten or fifteen of us?"

"No, not because of that, Barney, but because you could be makin' the damnedest mistake of your whole lousy life."

"And what about Martin's wife and kids?"

"Just settle down and when Sam gets back—"

"Sam! Why isn't he here? What's the town pay him for anyway!"

The elderly saddlemaker looked reprovingly at Sandal. "You're lettin' off steam is all," he muttered. "I figure Cliff's right. We'll get him—the feller who done that. But I figure we'd better not bust out over there to Mex-town and hang someone. Not yet anyway, Barney."

The saddlemaker went trudging unhappily over across the road.

Cliff stepped around the saloonman and walked inside, back to the doorway of the little unkempt office.

42

There was sticky dark blood on the floor, the safe door was ajar, papers were scattered and the three remaining men back there did not say a word as Cliff shouldered in and gazed at the devastation, then stepped carefully around the blood and went back as far as the dry-goods counter to sink down on one arm.

Had Alfonso really been hunting that mud-wagon when Cliff found him down along the creek, and if so why had he tried to do it in the dark? Unless, as he had said, he couldn't sleep and it had intrigued him, what Cliff had told him about the robbery of that man and his wife.

That man and his wife!

Cliff jerked up off the counter and walked quickly out of the store heading north, up past the saloon, the gunshop and the wagon-works towards the rooming-house.

FIVE
Suspicions

Sam Hart did not get back to his jailhouse office until dusk, but he had reached town an hour earlier. Saul Hanson had nailed him first, down at the barn, and after that at least six other people accosted him. He went over to the store, and a couple of townsmen trailed him in there too.

By the time he reached the office, where a lamp was burning, he knew as much as anyone knew of the robbery and killing. He stalked in, dusty and hungry and

43

tired, flung down his hat on the desktop and turned to get some water from the hanging *olla,* and saw his brother-in-law sitting perfectly still in a tipped-back chair along the north wall. He grunted, drank deeply, wiped his lips and did not speak until he had got to the chair behind his desk, sank down slowly, let his body loosen for the first time since early morning, then he said, "Where the hell you been; I looked high and low for you? Needed you to ride in a posse with me."

Cliff said, "Find anything?"

"No. Not a damned thing. Where was you?"

"Al Gutierrez and I found the mud-wagon."

Sheriff Hart stared. "Where?"

"About seven, eight miles below town hid in some creek willows." Cliff downed his chair with a sharp noise. "Sam, that feller and his wife are gone. Left last night, according to the lady who runs the rooming-house. They paid up until tomorrow, but they never slept in their beds last night."

"What of it?"

"Al and I did some tracking after sunup. We back-tracked the fellers from the mud-wagon to a place northeast of town, where two riders come out from here and met them."

Sheriff Hart's broad, wide forehead curled into three deep creases. His eyes did not waver nor blink as he studied Stanton. "Let's have the rest of it," he said, and folded big arms behind his head.

"To start off—they never got shoved off that coach at four in the morning, or they'd have been here in town

44

earlier than they got here. They was put off about mid-night, and my guess the reason for that was because they was to scout up Centreville. Sure, they showed up to you after daybreak, but I'll lay you odds they was around here hours and hours before that."

Sam's creased brow became a deep scowl. "You are saying they was—"

"I don't know. I don't know what they was up to, but they left town last night after dark, on horses they didn't have when they arrived here, and the tracks Al and I back-tracked came from town. I realize it don't make much sense—folks who've been robbed by stagers, riding out to meet the same fellers who robbed them . . . Unless those folks was never robbed at all; unless they was here in town to look over Martin's store and find his safe. And even then it don't make too much sense because how would they know he even had a safe, or that there'd be money in it? Unless, maybe, they've been through Centreville before, listened around, and found out folks usually put their greenbacks there because it's the biggest safe in town."

Sam kept staring at his brother-in-law, hands clasped behind his head. "What about the mud-wagon? Whoever heard of outlaws usin' a stage?"

Cliff fished around for his tobacco sack as he said, "I don't know a blessed thing more than I just told you. And most of that I made up after Al and I got back, and found out what happened . . . And you'd better corral Barney Sandal. He's tryin' to whip up a lynching bee

45

for Gutierrez. I damn near punched him in the nose in front of the store couple hours back. He's loaded for a hanging, Sam."

Sheriff Hart snorted. "He's not going to hang anyone." Sam brought his arms down, leaned forward upon the desk and waited until Cliff had lighted up, then he said, "Where those tracks from town met the other sign—which way did they go after that?"

"Looked like toward the mountains, but Al and I came on back. We'd been a long time without anything to eat. And I was beginnin' to worry a little about his back bothering him. We did a lot of horsebacking today."

"Cliff . . . ?"

"What?"

"Would you know Al Gutierrez's knife if you saw it?" Stanton blew smoke and gazed steadily at Sam Hart for a long moment before replying. "No, I wouldn't know his knife. But I know *him.* You've been listening to the talk Barney started."

Sheriff Hart continued to lean on the desktop. "Sure I been listening. To everyone who nailed me after I got back. But that don't mean I believe half of it."

Cliff blew smoke. "You want to head for the mountains?"

"Now? Gawdammit I just got back and my butt's dragging." Sheriff Hart groaned and rocked back. "It's dark out, Cliff."

"Yeah, I know. I also figure something else. If we don't figure some way to get on that trail those people

46

are going to be clean out of the country by tomorrow."

"They'll camp tonight—*if* they're the ones we got to catch."

"All the better to surprise them, Sam. If we ride out right now, on fresh stock . . ." Cliff trickled smoke and studied his brother-in-law.

Sheriff Hart lurched up out of his chair and went to the iron stove to slosh his graniteware coffeepot. It was half full of the same coffee which had been in there for almost a week. He stooped to poke in some paper and kindling, light it, then turned with a hang-dog expression. "In the morning," he muttered. "I'm whipped down to a frazzle."

Cliff nodded. "All right. Might be better if you stayed around town anyway. Keep Sandal and the other hot-headed idiots from doing something real bad over in Mex-town."

Sam snorted. "I told you—he's not going to do anything. Barney gets all fired up and sounds off a lot, but he's not dangerous."

"He was this evening, Sam, and he still will be tomorrow." Cliff arose and crossed over to pitch his cigarette butt into the crackling little stove. "I'll take Al with me tonight," he announced quietly. When he turned Sam Hart was staring at him.

"Cliff, wait until morning. You can't find the seat of your britches as dark as it is out tonight. Those folks can't neither. If they reach the hills."

"That's open country from here to those hills, Sam. They'll be able to see us coming after sunup, and they'll darned well realize it's trouble." Cliff went to the door and hung there briefly, one hand upon the latch. "If Al's out of town Barney'll have to find some other Mexican to hang."

Sam swore. "Damn it all; there's not going to be any hanging I told you! If Barney tries it I'll lock him up and throw away the key."

Cliff nodded and walked back out into the star-washed, balmy night.

Main Street had as many lights showing this night as usually only showed around Christmas time. A stream of men moved in and out of Sandal's saloon up the roadway and across it. Cliff shook his head, hitched at his gunbelt and struck out for the alleyway which led over to Mex-town.

The mud house was weakly lighted by six candles in dishes when Cliff walked in—and halted in embarrassment. That very pretty, slim Mexican woman was sitting at the table talking to Al Gutierrez. It was too gloomy in there to notice, but Cliff got red in the face. He said, "I'm sorry, Al. I thought you'd be alone."

The handsome woman arose. She stared from Cliff to his holstered Colt as though she were poised for flight. He had noticed that in her before, when she had first appeared at the *jacal*. He offered a reassurance. "I should have knocked first, lady. I'll leave and come back a little later."

Alfonso sat watching them both, and when the pretty woman spoke to him, Al gravely nodded. She whisked around Cliff, disappearing into the darkness beyond.

Al looked after her and sighed. Then he said, "Close the door, *compadre.*"

Cliff ignored the ajar door at his back. "Did she tell you what they been sayin' around town?"

Alfonso nodded. "You ever see me wear *huarachas,* Cliff? Nobody else has either. That's *peon* stuff. I been wearin' boots since I first worked for the Morgans and got paid enough to buy a pair . . . The knife?" Al jerked his head tiredly in the direction of a shelf beside his little iron stove. "It's there. They all look pretty much alike anyway." He faced Cliff. "Is Sam back?"

"Yeah."

Cliff went to the bench the pretty Mexican woman had abandoned, sat down and said, "That man and woman who said they'd been robbed by those stagers in the mud-wagon, left town sometime last night, or maybe early this morning. Al, I'll lay you big odds that's whose tracks came east from town and met up with those four fellers from the mud-wagon we tracked up here."

Gutierrez gazed at his friend as candles waved gently from a light breeze coming through the doorway. He arose, closed the door, resumed his seat and said, *"They* killed Martin?"

Cliff shrugged. "I don't know who killed him. I know who *didn't* kill him."

Gutierrez showed perfect white teeth in a thin and humorless small smile. *"Gracias, amigo."*

"Can you climb back atop a horse tonight, Al?"

Gutierrez blinked. "Tonight? Why tonight?"

49

"I'm going to ride to the foothills and be up there come daybreak to find the sign of those people."

Gutierrez did not offer the objection Cliff's brother-in-law had offered—about not riding in the darkness—he simply sat a while gazing across the table, before slowly shaking his head. "I can't make it. I didn't tell you this afternoon but the last couple hours my legs went numb and my back hurt. That's what *she* was giving me hell about before you walked in; even riding out this morning. Cliff; I'd never make it all the way to the foothills. I'd have to pile off and sit under a tree for a while."

Gutierrez seemed so apologetic that Cliff smiled at him. "It don't matter a whole lot."

Alfonso kept studying his friend's face. "You wanted me out of town. No?"

That indeed had been part of it. "Yeah, I suppose so."

"I know what Barney Sandal's trying to do. She wasn't the only person came by this afternoon to tell me of things. He wants to lynch me for Martin's murder."

Cliff was embarrassed for some reason. "He's not going to hang anyone. Sam said that. Sam's going to corral him and settle him down. And anyone else thinks they're going to cause trouble."

Al's brows climbed. "Sam's not going with you?"

Cliff shook his head without explaining.

For a moment Gutierrez sat gazing across the table in calm thought, then he said, "I'll tell you who I'd take along if I was in your boots."

50

"Who?"

"Barney Sandal."

They looked at one another until Alfonso made that thin, humorless small smile again, then Cliff laughed. The first time anything had really seemed funny to him in a long time. "I think you're right. You want to know something, Al? You folks really are sort of slippery at that."

Gutierrez's smile deepened and broadened. "Us greasers?"

"Naw. I didn't say that . . . That's always hit me as a sort of mean thing to say about Mexicans." Cliff's eyes twinkled. "How about—beaners?"

Gutierrez nodded. "Or pepper-bellies. I've heard them all. Only one of them bothers me . . . You want some coffee with tequila in it?"

Cliff shrugged. "Sure." He didn't want even the coffee, actually, and he had never been able to abide tequila. It was worse than that brandy Barney had brought back from Raton one time.

He sat in thought while Gutierrez went to the little iron stove. When Gutierrez returned with a pair of dented tin cups filled to the brim and said, "You'd better drink that down and get on your way." Cliff lifted the cup, tasted, made a horrible face and set the coffee down. It wasn't the tequila, which was scarcely notice-able, it was the coffee.

"I'm in no hurry," he told Alfonso. "I got to catch Barney after he locks up. I can't just barge in there and yank him out from behind the bar." He tried the coffee again. Either his gullet was numb or the stuff wasn't really that bad. He drank part of it before saying, "Who was she, Al?"

Gutierrez answered without hesitation. "Juana Sanchez. You remember a man named Sanchez who worked for Lew Calkins at the saddle shop a few years back?"

"Yeah. His daughter?"

"Yes."

Cliff tried the coffee again. This time it tasted good. He finished the cup and shoved it away. "You going to marry her? You should; she's sure pretty."

Gutierrez avoided a direct answer. "More coffee?"

"No thanks." Cliff leaned to arise. "I figured you'd ought to marry her."

Gutierrez still said nothing, but he sighed a little and also arose to see his friend to the door. Over there, he offered some advice. "Be damned careful. Not just in front, but don't let Sandal get behind you."

"I'll watch the bastard," conceded Cliff, and stepped outside into the warm and very pleasant night. "And you—if I was you'd I'd sort of stay out of *gringo*-town tomorrow. Sam won't let anything happen, but all the same. . . ."

Alfonso understood.

Cliff winked and turned back in the direction of that crooked little alleyway which connected Mex-town and *gringo*-town. Overhead, there were millions too many stars to count. There had been a fitful little warm desert breeze earlier, coming up from the south-

52

country, but now it was as still as death all around, and for once the middle of town, up around the saloon was even quiet.

Cliff leaned in overhanging-darkness out front of the saddle shop, had a smoke while watching the saloon, and decided that tequila he'd drunk back yonder wasn't as bad as he had expected it to be, and he never had liked the stuff.

SIX
Beyond The Darkness

Barney was mad, but because he was not a sulky person he had plenty to say, all of it salted with hair-raising profanity. They were a mile up the north coachroad when he paused, glared, then asked a question.

"Would you have pulled that damned trigger on me?"

Cliff gazed back. "You'll never know, will you? Why don't you just shut up and ride."

"You're crazy," stated the angry saloonman, pulling his neck lower into his riding coat. "Crazy as a darned coot. You're not going to find those people in the damned night."

Cliff said nothing. They were side-by-side and the road stretched ahead like a silver ribbon. There was no moon but there was a lot of starshine. It was not as good as moonlight, but it was a lot better than no light at all.

Cliff did not feel tired, for some reason. He had felt

that way when they had first returned, he and Al Gutierrez. Maybe a meal at Will's cafe had helped, and maybe too that slug of tequila in the coffee had helped. As a matter of fact, after so many years of pre-dawn risings and late-night retirings, Cliff had become adjusted to a lot less sleep than most people, but that only accounted for his lack of drowsiness. The human carcass got tired in other ways; in the muscles and joints, in the backbone and the behind after six or eight hours of saddle-backing. But he was tough and sinewy and durable.

He said, "Barney; did you ever hear tell that tequila has medicinal qualities?"

"Has what?"

"Works on folks like medicine."

Sandal snorted. "It works on folks all right, but not like any medicine I ever taken." He turned his head. "You been drinkin' that stuff?"

"One jolt in black coffee."

"Sure. Over in Mex-town with your greaser friends."

Cliff let his breath out slowly before saying, "You ever see Mex blood?"

"No. And what of it?"

"It's red too, Barney. You ever see a little Mex kid cry? The tears look just like ours. You ever see a real pretty Mex woman?"

"Oh for Chris'zake," groaned the saloonman, and deliberately peered dead ahead up the roadway. "This is a darned set of foolishness, riding out like this, in the darned darkness!"

Cliff waited another mile before fishing in his coat pocket, lifting out the bullets and handing them over. "Now you can load that gun again," he said.

Sandal looked as though he might refuse, then he snatched away the ammunition, reached inside his coat for the empty gun and as he fiercely punched the slugs in he said, "And I'd ought to use some of it on you. Did you know it's against the law, stealin' folks at gunpoint? Wait until Sam—"

"Turn off the road, Barney. We'll head east for a while."

Sandal was still loading the gun so he had to make the shift awkwardly and that set him to cursing again. But he remained beside his companion, although he sounded derisive when he said, "Now you're goin' to tell me you got second-sight or something. How do you know they went over this way? They more'n likely turned west, or went straight up into the mountains."

Cliff was patient. He usually was. "When Al Gutierrez and I last saw their sign, back where they met up with that feller and his wife from town, they were commencing to angle off easterly."

"You think they couldn't do something like that just to throw folks off? How would you act, after you robbed a town and killed a feller, and knew damned well your tracks would be all over?"

Cliff eyed the saloonman in thoughtful silence. If Barney was thinking like that, it meant he was beginning to suspect Cliff might be right; might not be as crazy as he had seemed back in town when he had stepped out of that dog-trot between two buildings with a gun in his fist.

"We'll take a chance on bein' right," he mildly stated.

The night was advancing and although it would not be a cold one, not until an hour or so just ahead of sunrise, that earlier balminess was beginning to dissipate. This was how Cliff estimated the time. He owned a watch but it was back at his house in town. He guessed it was a little past midnight, maybe about one o'clock in the morning, when they heard dogs barking south of them in the middle distance.

Barney spoke from low in his coat-collar. "Morgan place; they got ten dozen dogs over there all the time. Wors'n an In'ian camp."

Cliff knew where they were. He was also making some assessments about the probable, or at least the *possible,* route those outlaws had taken and about where they would strike the first low foothills which lay still a couple of miles northward. He set a fresh course so as to be along those foothills when dawnlight arrived.

According to his knowledge of the country, and the possible route of those riders up ahead, once the strangers got close enough to the foothills they had to either enter them for cover, or parallel them out on the grassland to avoid rocks and spiny underbrush farther back. Riding at night with poor visibility, he reckoned they would avoid the foothills and merely parallel them, at least until daybreak when they would need cover, and when they could also see around well enough to navigate the foothills.

What he wanted more than to find those people, was to come across their sign. If, as Barney had said, they had changed course back somewhere to delay pursuit, then he was going to feel bad, and to Barney Sandal, he was going to look bad. Also, if they had been riding in the opposite direction all night, they were not going to be able to back-track and pick up the correct trail without a big loss of time.

Barney could have told him most of this. Instead, he blew on his hands from time to time, looked ahead and to their left towards the foothills, and kept silent.

Not until the sound of those barking dogs had dropped to a very faint echo, did Barney say anything more. Then he poked his head up out of the coat-collar, like a big unhappy turtle, and scowled. "Just how far do you expect they got to? We could be by-passin' them up here, Cliff."

They had been walking the horses. It may have seemed to someone who had spent a large part of his mature life behind bars that they had covered a lot of territory, but they hadn't and Cliff knew it.

"We'll go another couple of miles then haul up and wait for daylight, Barney. You cold?"

"Cold? Me? No; whatever made you think that? I always ride horseback in the shank of the night with a coat buttoned up to my ears. It's just something I do is all."

Cliff softly laughed, then turned. "I'll tell you something. I damned near punched you in the nose out front of the store this afternoon."

"*Yesterday* afternoon. And if you had I'd have punched your head soft!"

Cliff decided that although the anger had turned to indignation, Barney Sandal was not yet in quite the mood for them to talk. Then a horse whinnied up ahead and northward and they both yanked back. Cliff stepped to earth with a fluid motion and placed a light hand over the nostrils of the animal he was riding. Barney did not do that right away, but he did it finally, just in case the horse decided to whinny back.

There was not another sound until Barney belatedly said, "Damned loose-stock."

Maybe. Maybe not. Cliff decided that when the odds were six-to-one and he was out there in exposed, open country with Barney, it would be foolish to take a chance. He handed Sandal his reins, stooped to shuck his spurs, and as he arose to move off he said, "Keep them quiet."

Barney nodded without opening his mouth, but a few moments after Cliff was lost ahead in the darkness Barney unbuttoned the lower part of his coat, tucked it back and tugged loose the tie-down thong over his Colt, and swore.

Cliff knew they were close to the foothills; maybe a mile or three-quarters of a mile away from them. He also knew that if it was loose-stock and they had picked up the scent of the horses Barney was holding out there, they would probably go ambling down there to investigate. He stopped once, sank belly-down to press an ear to the earth, heard nothing, picked up no reverberations, and arose with fresh caution as he slipped ahead again.

The first horse he saw, also saw him, or scented him. It was standing like a stone, little ears ahead, peering directly into the ghostly starlight down where Cliff had halted. Two other horses hopped up and also stood staring.

Somewhere, farther back, a man cleared his pipes and lustily expectorated. Cliff fixed the location of that man, then watched as another pair of horses hopped up. They were constricted at the pasterns with those figure-eight leather hobbles rangemen called "Mormon hobbles".

One horse, more curious and less timid than the others, made a couple more little hops towards Cliff, head and neck extended.

Cliff saw the "M" on his left shoulder, a neat, clear brand. He walked very slowly over to get on the left side of the other animals. They all had the same mark in the same place.

Up where that man had noisily roused, someone was muttering, and within moments a thin, upright tongue of flame came to life. Against this feeble brilliance Cliff could discern the hunkering figure. The hat was askew, there was awry hair sticking from beneath it on both sides, and as the man turned to rummage in a pannier, very obligingly exposing most of his face as the breakfast-fire brisked up steadily casting light farther out, Cliff grunted.

That man was Jess Turnbow, top-hand for the Morgans. Cliff relaxed slightly looking around. It was a cow-camp, there were three lumpy bedrolls scattered around amid mounds of saddlery.

Cliff walked closer, then whistled to make his presence known, and proceeded on up where Turnbow, standing erect now with a hand on his holstered Colt, was waiting with an unsmiling expression over his stubbly bronzed features.

Cliff smiled. " 'Morning, Jess."

Turnbow loosened. " 'Morning, Cliff. If you're up here for the fishin' it's the wrong day of the week—an' awful early in the morning." The rangeman looked elsewhere. "You alone?"

"No. Barney Sandal's back yonder holding our horses."

"Barney? . . . What in hell are you two fellers up to, Cliff?"

"We're lookin' for five men and a woman riding up through here somewhere, Jess."

Turnbow turned briefly when his fire spat sparks and loudly crackled. As this disruption diminished he looked back. "In the night, headin' east?"

"Likely. You see them?"

Jess Turnbow shook his head. "Hell no. It was plumb dark. We'd just soaked the coals and had turned in. But we heard them. Wasn't loose-stock nor cattle so it had to be riders. We sort of wondered. This isn't no roadway up here. Mister Morgan don't like too much trespassing. If it hadn't be so darned late and we'd been cattle-hunting in the mountains since dawn we might have gone after them . . . Who was they?"

Instead of an immediate reply Cliff explained about the killing and robbery in town. Turnbow's mouth hung slack. Those listening men farther back were sitting up in their blankets. One of them said, "Martin Hamm? I'll be double damned."

Turnbow finally found his tongue. "And you figure those strangers had a hand in it? Hey, Cliff, wait until I get outside some coffee and I'll help you hunt down them people."

Barney came trudging in through the brightening pre-dawn cold morning, leading the horses. "Heard you talking," he announced, and stepped past to hold his hands to the fire.

The riders were scrambling from their bedrolls, groping for britches, shirts, hats and boots. One of them spoke with a high voice. "Barney; you don't look the same in fresh air."

The other two laughed and Sandal stonily ignored them all to continue soaking up heat.

Cliff was concerned with how far ahead those outlaws were. Jess had to mull over an answer before offering it.

"If they camped last night, I'd say maybe not more'n about five, six miles. Seven at the most. If they pushed along . . . I sure would in their boots; I wouldn't stop until I was in Messico—anyway, if they kept going, they might be a hell of a lot farther. It would depend on their livestock, wouldn't it?"

That high-voiced rangerider came over. He was a twig of a man, but tall and that only made his thinness more noticeable. In the high voice he said, "Let's go. I'll fetch in the horses."

Jess considered the man and began to scowl. "We didn't find all those damned steers, you know."

The cowboy, like all of his kind, was perfectly willing to forget everything and go on a manhunt. "We can pick them up on the way back, Jess."

Turnbow had reached his decision. "You fellers keep on ferreting them out and take them to the ranch. I'll go with Cliff and Barney. Just me."

The thin man looked steadily at Jess, giving the impression he might not obey. Behind him, a heavier, older rider said, "That's what we'll do, Lennie."

The thin rangerider slumped, muttered under his breath and turned back to hunt a tin cup and swab it with grass, then to see if the fire was hot enough now to put on the pan for their coffee.

Barney owlishly watched all of them, unwilling to back away from the heat even when Lennie came around to his side to tether the coffee pan atop two flat stones.

Dawn was coming. There would be fish-belly gray-ness first, for about an hour, then there would be a pale goldness, and finally the sun would pop up over the eastern rims. The sky which had been cloudless in the night, would also be cloudless this fresh new day.

SEVEN
Toward Sunrise

They had coffee first, both Jess and Barney insisted upon it and Cliff became resigned. If they were as close as five miles to those people he wanted to get on with it; get up there and get it over with. He had no clear idea what he would do when he found those people but he wanted to face them anyway. After that, it would be largely up to them what happened next.

As they were riding off that thin cowboy looked resentfully after them and muttered under his breath. The other riders ignored him.

Jess Turnbow had been riding Morgan-country for six years and as extensive as it was there were very few parts of it he did not know as well as he knew the back of his hand.

But he did not lead Cliff and Barney easterly along the foothills, without explaining what to him should have been obvious, he took them up a brush-free slot in the crumbly lower hills, arrow-straight along a sloping sidehill and through a stand of scrub-pine to a distant plateau which had chaparral as high as a horse's back and full of prickly thorns. By then the visibility had increased, and so had the cold.

Barney rode like a big turtle, hunkering down inside his riding coat, his face doggedly set in an expression of thorough unhappiness.

Jess halted, scratched, looked eastward and slowly raised a gloved hand.

"Yonder."

All Cliff made out was some horses just inside the environs of the lower foothills. They looked to him as though they were loose-stock; they were fairly well bunched and were peacefully grazing.

Barney saw them this way too, and said, "That's just horses, Cliff."

Turnbow cast a sardonic smile towards the saloonman. "Not ours, if they is, Barney. We only got loose-stock five, six miles westerly, and down south on the horse-range."

"They could come up here. What's to stop them?"

Jess did not answer. Horses did not travel that far that fast, especially in the darkness, unless something had spooked hell out of them, and if they had been south-westerly they would have run, not for the mountains, but for familiar country down where they had been. But Barney was a townsman.

Jess eased out, taking them down the far side of that pleasant plateau into some stands of timber which had stumps here and there where firewood-cutters had left wagon-tracks.

The sun was coming. There was a pale blaze of pinkish light along the easterly distances which reached that grassy place where those horses were grazing. It had not quite reached back where Jess was riding with his companions but it shortly would, and Barney Sandal for one would not be unhappy when it got that far; the others might be inured to exposure, especially this early in the morning, but he wasn't. The inside of a saloon was warm day and night—and even in the early morning, but Barney hadn't been up this early in more years than he cared to think back on.

Jess knew what he was doing. He also knew where he was going and kept plenty of hillsides between himself, his companions, and that lower area where those horses had been seen. He said very little as he rode, and that was agreeable with Cliff. Barney, in the rear, might have grumbled if there had been anyone back there to grumble to.

They made a sashay out and around a stand of dark timber, then went southward again to pick up the rough line of direct approach and when Jess was satisfied, he halted without a word to the others until they too had dismounted to loop reins among low pine limbs, then he cocked a squinty look skyward and said, "They must be dog-tired to still be in camp after sunrise."

Barney, for once, said something the other two could ponder. "Or too smart to head out until they're damned sure no one's coming across country after them."

Jess went unerringly southward now, on foot, his spurs making a dull, musical sound as he walked through the total stillness.

They had covered enough miles, Cliff speculated, to be roughly above, or behind, those horses. He wished they could have made a closer top-out to make certain those were not, as Barney had surmised, just some loose horses. But Jess's confidence was reassuring—in a way. Cliff left the tie-down on his Colt hanging free as he moved along behind the Morgan-rider.

Where Jess finally stopped and held up a hand for silence, they were behind a flat-topped low, rocky escarpment. Several trees that looked to Cliff like fat junipers were up there, pale needles somber against the brightening sky.

The sun was up, now, but down where they stood behind the shale-rock hill it was still gray and cold. Barney rubbed palms together and peered left and right. When Jess started up the rocky hill Barney sighed; this was something else he was unaccustomed to—climbing.

When they got up there Barney hid from the others the fact that he was panting like a young bull in a corralful of heifers.

Jess sank to one knee among those diaper-scented fat little pale trees. When Cliff came beside him and saw the camp—as much of it as was visible because it was tucked back in against a sidehill—he softly said, "All right. If it's not them. . . ."

Barney, hunkering on Cliff's far side, suddenly pointed. A woman had just walked over where two men were drinking coffee beside a dry-wood fire which sent up no smoke, only heat. "Not too many women on cow-ranges this far from towns, with rangemen."

It was meant to be sarcastic, but it came out as a plain statement of fact.

Cliff had never met any of those people, but he was inclined to agree with Barney's judgment. Jess

66

Turnbow swung his gaze out and around, making a general's appraisal of the best way to get down where those strangers were. When he finally spoke he said, "If we can get between them and their livestock, we got 'em."

But out where the horses were grazing there was nothing but grassland. Not even any underbrush. Cliff's thoughts brushed that aside because it was impossible. "Just take us around that sidehill where they got their camp, without any noise, Jesse."

Turnbow arose, moved back behind the little fat trees, glanced over where Barney was just now arising, stiffly and complainingly, shot Cliff a look and wagged his head, then struck out.

The distance was not great but getting around that sidehill where even the brush was stunted because of a thin overlay of nourishing soil above solid rock, posed a problem, and Jesse halted when they were close enough to pick up the smell of fire and coffee, speculated about how to proceed, then moved out again, more slowly from here on.

They had to hunch part of the way. They also had to scheme ahead to be certain they would not be exposed. If there was trouble, they were up there against that sunlighted sidehill like crows on a fence—perfect targets.

Barney almost slipped in some tallis-rock and Jess turned on him with a savage look, but Barney had grabbed a handful of bush-limbs to prevent a fall so the loose stones underfoot merely shifted, they did not go down-slope in a rattling small landslide.

When they started onward Barney cursed to himself in a whisper and picked tiny thorns from the palm of his left hand. But from here on he did as the others were doing, he placed one foot probingly ahead of the other foot in order not to repeat his near disaster.

They got over into the last clump of buck-brush and squatted. Below and slightly to their right, southward, they had the camp, the cooking-fire, the people and even the more distant horses, in plain sight.

Cliff leaned towards Jess. "One bullet in the grass out yonder and we'll have them on foot."

Jess did not respond for a moment, then he said, "Yeah, and then those fellers will have us pinned on this lousy slope, too, like ducks on a pond."

Barney crept closer to hear better. "All we got to do is for me to go stumblin' down there and say I got lost last night in the hills when my horse run off. . . . And get the drop on them."

Cliff and Jess gazed at the burly man in his old coat and battered hat. It might work at that. It could be true; something about like it was happening every day some-where in mountainous country. Except that Barney was no hand with a six-gun, and if he didn't get his six-gun caught in his coat, he probably wouldn't be fast enough with it anyway. Then they would kill him.

There were five men down there. Even from this dis-tance it was easy to see that they were not novices. They had hip-holstered six-guns and back where the horse-gear was lying were booted Winchesters. To Cliff, who had faced outlaws during his staging days,

68

this crew looked experienced and deadly. He shook his head at Barney.

"They'll have you for breakfast."

Jess Turnbow rubbed his unshaven jaw, spat aside and settled for a long study of the situation. Two of the men down where sunlight was just beginning to add new-day warmth, had their backs to the slope. Another man had walked out for dead-fall wood and returned with an armload of it to feed the fire. The fourth man was hiking back northward where there was thick underbrush and several pine trees, and the fifth man was talking to the woman. Cliff guessed who that fifth man was by his little curly-brimmed derby hat and his gray matching britches and coat; the fellow who had been back in town with the woman he was now talking to.

All Cliff could make out about the woman was that she was lean and sharp-featured and was wearing a gray dress about the same color as the man's suit. She could have been twenty or fifty. She was about average height and build for a female, and she had brown hair coiled in back under a brimless hat the same color as her dress. If she was armed there was no way to determine that from this distance, and maybe even up close there would be no way to determine it—by looking, anyway.

Jess finally shook his head. "We better wait until they fetch in the horses and are rigging up. That way they'll be busy and we can get a better chance."

The heat was finally beginning to wash over

everyone with a pleasant variety of warmth which was still not quite enough to loosen night-chilled muscles and joints but it was certainly an improvement. Even Barney finally loosened the gullet of his coat and stopped rubbing his hands together.

He leaned towards Cliff. "My maw wanted me to be a blacksmith. Good pay and you're warm by a forge most of the time. I should have listened to her. Then I wouldn't be out here this morning, I'd be stoking up a nice fire somewhere in town."

Cliff grinned. "Naw. By now, Barney, some mule would have kicked you in the head and you'd be wanderin' around trying to remember where you left your hat."

Jess ignored them to steadily assess their situation. In his line of work a man learned early to think well ahead. That was the difference between top-hands and men like that thin, lanky cowboy back yonder called Lennie. When he finally saw two of those strangers leave the fire with ropes, he was satisfied they were nearing the time for a showdown. He looked elsewhere, but the best cover within safe distance was exactly where they were squatting. He would have much preferred being behind stone, but there was nothing but that substantial upthrusting from this particular sidehill.

He leaned to quietly say, "Bunched up like this all they got to do is figure where we are and blow all three of us to kingdom come. Crawl off a little ways, leave plenty of space between us."

No one moved right away. Barney scowled at Jess. "You want to make a war of it?"

Jess got irritable. "No, I don't want to make no war of it, damn it, but the minute they know we're up here *they're* going to, Barney. You better bet your last *peso* on that!"

"I still think I could just go stumblin' down there and—"

"Spread out," said Cliff, not wishing to have an argument start right now. "Barney, be quiet; look where you're crawling."

Jess stayed in place. Cliff and Barney crept northward until they were about five yards from Jess, then Barney kept crawling to get roughly the same distance between himself and Cliff.

The sun rose higher and struck them in the eyes. Barney pulled his hat forward and low, lifted out his Colt and swore about the same sunshine he had been waiting all night for.

EIGHT
Fight!

Cliff was watching those two outlaws heading for the horses when Jess twisted and hissed, then wigwagged with his six-gun. Cliff nodded understanding. He was satisfied; they were about ready to start things.

The woman went to the fire and stood alone for a long time with a tin cup of coffee, gazing around, and finally turning towards those men who had gone for the horses.

To Cliff, she seemed very calm and collected, as though perhaps she were another Belle Starr or Calamity Jane; that kind of woman to whom the outlaw trail was preferable to tamer living. There were a few like that, Cliff knew, although he had never before seen one this close.

One man turned from the camp as though he might have heard something up the westward slope. Cliff held his breath. No one had made a sound up there. Maybe the outlaw hadn't heard anything, maybe it was something he had seen; sunlight bouncing off a six-gun barrel for example.

Then the man turned and called to a companion across the tangled pile of flung-aside horse equipment. "I'll climb that slope and look around, Eb."

Eb did not seem very interested. "Won't be necessary. We're goin' back into the mountains from here and directly we'll be able to see back down yonder anyway, and up there ain't nobody going to find us."

The first man answered quickly. "We left enough sign for a blind man to foller." He turned towards the sidehill and Cliff glanced over where Jess was lying. The top-hand had just very gently eased back the hammer of his Colt. That outlaw was never going to make it more than halfway up.

The woman turned and said something to the man in the curly-brimmed little hat. He glanced over his shoulder where the other outlaw was starting for the sidehill.

"Charley," he called. "Forget it. We're ready to rig out. We don't need to be delayed."

72

The man was near the base of the slope when he halted and looked around at the man in the gray suit. Without a word he turned back.

They were bringing in the horses now, so everyone but the woman headed for that tangle of horse gear. The woman continued to leisurely sip her coffee. She seemed to Cliff Stanton to be perfectly at ease. He was fascinated by her.

Jess fidgeted to get closer to the impenetrable base of his thorny, sprawling buck-brush. The only thing to be said for that bush, for all the bushes around here for many yards, was that no one could see through them, down low. But they would not turn a bullet; they would not even delay the passage of one.

Those men down there had Winchesters. The three men upon the slope had only six-guns. The range was adequate but Cliff, for one, would have felt better with a Winchester. It was hard to say about Jess; rangemen rarely carried saddleguns; only when they went after cattle-killing bears, cougars, or maybe wolf packs. And sometimes, but rarely, after horsethieves and rustlers.

But wishing wasn't going to change anything so Cliff emulated Jess, he squeezed down lower and got in closer to his bush.

The outlaws were together, except for the woman who remained over by the fire with her tin cup of coffee. She seemed perfectly at home in this environment, but her dress and that little gray hat were totally out of place. She did not even look like a ranch-woman; she was dressed for town.

Jess turned slowly. Cliff caught the movement. Jess pointed down the slope and slowly bobbed his head to signify the time was rife. Cliff turned, but Barney had already seen Jess's signal and had correctly interpreted it. Barney had his gloves off, his six-gun in his right hand, and his hatbrim tugged low.

One of the horses being saddled lay back his ears, bared big yellow teeth and squealed the way cinchy horses frequently did. The man turned to look ahead, to growl at the animal as he braced to take another tug, and up the slope Jess Turnbow's raised six-gun caught sunlight with a cold gray brilliance. The outlaw did not even yell, he jumped away from his horse and dived head-first towards the nearest shelter which was a mound of saddlery and rolled blankets. Then he fired up the hill.

The other men were stunned, but only for seconds; they were wary by habit and alert by nature. They turned to scatter. One of them grabbed at a carbine-butt sticking out of the gear as he darted. Barney fired at him. The stock of that carbine exploded into splinters and the man went down rolling over and over clutching a hand and wrist which sprayed blood.

The outlaw behind the equipment tried a blind shot in the direction from which Barney had fired. Jess deliberately eased around his bush, aimed coolly and fired. He hit that downhill gunman directly through the head. The man fell back flat, then kicked and jerked.

Cliff saw the woman drop her tin cup and turn to flee. Her panic drove her directly out across the open country where those horses had been grazing. She would have been an easy target for the first fifty yards, but no one tried to bring her down, and after that she was out of six-gun range. But she was running, holding up her long skirt with both hands.

Two outlaws called back and forth as they got against the down-slope into some underbrush. Cliff fired a sound-shot at the nearest one. The other one, north-ward, fired at Cliff's bush.

Barney was waiting for that. His shot sounded almost like a continuation of the shot the outlaw had thrown. Then Barney bracketed that man; fired to the left, to the right, and drove one right down the middle. The outlaw flopped over onto his back. His hat rolled a couple of feet away.

Jess knew where the other one was behind a bush. He waited, though, for shaky movement, then fired down into it. A man screamed, then went silent.

One outlaw was exposed from the knees down over near the horse equipment. He did not fire. In fact he had not fired at all when Cliff saw him raise his soiled old hat in a frantic wigwagging motion. Jess yelled to that man.

"Pitch the gun out!"

Without any delay a six-gun sailed over some bushes and landed in plain sight.

Another outlaw fiercely cursed his companion for giving up. Cliff fired at the sound. A thickly-made man arose unsteadily, turned and started slowly in the direction of the fire. Then fell belly-down and never moved again.

The man in the city clothes yelled up the hill. "That's enough. You fellows up there, that's enough!"

Jess was aiming towards that voice when Cliff said, "Give him a chance."

Jess nodded and kept his cocked six-gun aimed and ready. He had not intended to try and kill the dude, he just intended to be ready to.

Cliff yelled out. "Stand up. You in the gray pants, and you behind that horse-junk. Stand up!"

The gray-suited man obeyed but the other outlaw called back while still hiding. "Don't shoot. I already give up and tossed away the gun. Don't shoot. All right?"

Barney swore. "Stand up you son of a bitch, or I *will* shoot."

The outlaw obeyed, but he came up into a crouch first, poised for sudden movement. When nothing happened he got awkwardly upright and stood with both hands hanging at his sides. There was blood on his coat.

It was over. Cliff had sweat running inside his shirt and both palms were wet even though there was not yet enough sunlight-warmth to have caused any of this. He leaned back and systematically reloaded before watching Jess start down the hill.

The woman was gone into the trees across the meadow.

Cliff, who had felt calm, almost detached, throughout the sudden, savage fight, now finally saw what he and Barney and Jess had done. They had killed outright all

76

but the man in the derby hat, the man with the shattered wrist who was still writhing over where the grass around him was turning redder by the moment, and that other one, the one who had surrendered first, but even as he looked down there that one, the first to give up and pitch away his gun, lifted his coat, looked inside slowly, dropped the coat and slowly sat down. He did not look up even when Jess arose nor when Barney called to Jess to watch those men down there. As Cliff stared, the outlaw eased over onto his side and lay in the morning grass as though he were sleeping.

There were two survivors. The only one not to have been hit was the tall man in the derby hat. Jess slid down the hill, ignoring that outlaw, and strode over where the other was grinding his teeth in pain. Jess leaned and struck the outlaw over the head, then he holstered his Colt and knelt to go to work.

Cliff and Barney came down too. The dude stared at them, then over to Jess Turnbow, then back again. "Just you three?"

Cliff said, "Shove up your hands," and systematically searched. He found a derringer belly-gun and a Bowie knife. The belly-gun he had half-expected to find. The big curved knife lay in his hand for a moment while he gazed at its owner, then he flipped the weapon towards the dying fire and shook his head. "What's your name?" he demanded.

"Carl Sloat."

"What's the woman's name?"

"Virginia. Virginia Sloat."

"Your wife?"

"No. She's my sister."

Cliff holstered his six-gun. "Where did you get that knife and Mex sandal you left beside the storekeeper's body, Mister Sloat?"

"Well . . ."

Barney cocked his six-gun. He had killed and he was perfectly willing to do it again.

Carl Sloat looked at Barney and looked swiftly away. "From out back of a Mexican hut. The knife was sticking in a tabletop back there, beside some cheese and some round loaves of bread."

Cliff looked at Barney. "Satisfied? Here's your Mexican who killed Martin."

Instead of showing personal remorse, Barney shoved the cocked six-gun into the prisoner's middle. "I ought to blow you apart."

Cliff, who had seen an entirely new side of Barney Sandal since the fight had started, almost held his breath. He could not tell whether Barney would murder the dude or not.

"You knifed the storekeeper, then?" said Barney, and Carl Sloat was afraid to answer. He got white to the eyes as he stared at Sandal whose finger was curled around the trigger of that cocked Colt whose barrel was buried in his stomach.

Cliff took a chance. "Let him be, Barney. Sure he killed Martin, and we're going to take him back for that. Don't shoot the bastard, he's not worth the mess it'd land you in."

Jess called. "One of you fellers lend me a hand."

Neither of them moved until Cliff gestured for Barney to go over where Jess was down on both knees, hands and wrists stained with blood. Barney went, obeying the order for some reason. He was not a man who normally took orders in good grace.

Carl Sloat relaxed slightly and said, "Thanks. I think he might have done it."

Cliff eyed the man coldly. "They'll do it down in town. Legal-like . . . What time did you folks reach town the other night—and don't tell me it was any four o'clock in the morning."

The prisoner seemed almost completely at ease with Cliff Stanton when he answered. "About one o'clock."

"And you scouted up the place."

Sloat nodded. He was a dark-eyed man with the same thin features his sister had. He did not look dangerous but no one who carried a belly-gun was not dangerous.

"How did you get the storekeeper out of his house in the night?"

"He was already outside, mister. And that's all I'm going to say."

Cliff considered, then swung with surprising speed. Sloat went over backwards, struck the ground with a trickle of flung-back blood upwards across his cheek from a broken lip.

Barney returned, groping under his coat for the six-gun. Sloat started to struggle to his feet. He had been dazed but he had never lost consciousness. Cliff had not struck that hard. When Sloat saw Barney raising the

79

gun he struggled to spit words through smashed lips.

"Wait. I'll explain it. You—don't let him shoot me!"

Cliff neither moved nor spoke. He waited for Barney to pull the trigger. From back farther Jess said, "Don't kill the bastard, Barney. I don't think this one's going to make it and we got to have one of them who can talk."

Barney wavered, his gun rigidly pointing downward, his coarse features twisted into an expression of pure hatred.

To perhaps tip the scales in favor of the dude, Cliff repeated his question. "How did you catch the store-keeper?"

Words spurted from the downed man. "He was out back. We went through the alley to find his house, and he was just leaving the outhouse. Someone was. We didn't know who for certain until I caught him between there and the main house. It was him all right. I knew him from another time we were in Centreville."

"And?" prompted Cliff.

"And—we took him to the store with a gun in his back. He opened the safe and tried to argue. . . ."

"And you knifed him," said Cliff. "And tossed down that Mex sandal and the knife."

"I—left the knife sticking in—him."

Jess walked over wiping off blood with someone's soiled neckerchief. He looked at the prisoner's bleeding, swelling lips and said, "Why don't you fellers load the son of a bitch on a horse so we can get down where this other one can get looked after. His gun-hand and wrist are all peppered to hell with fragments of a lead slug and wood splinters. He's lost a heap of blood."

Barney was skeptical. "No one dies from something that far from their heart."

Jess ignored Barney until the saloonman said, "What about the woman?" then Jess glanced almost indifferently over where they had last seen Virginia Sloat. "She won't get far," he replied to Barney. "Not over there. We'll get her."

They had to go back for their own horses so Barney was assigned this task and for once he did not bitterly squawk. The horses which the outlaws had been rigging out had broken to the four winds after the first furious exchange of gunfire. They would no doubt be caught later by Morgan-riders, but that would not help the three men from Centreville right now.

They worked in silence bundling the dead, which would have to be left until someone could return for them. They found six buckskin pouches of gold and silver on the saddlebags. They also found a stack of greenbacks, evidently from the till at the general store, and these had been hastily tied with a scrap of dirty string. They had no idea how much money had come from Martin Hamm's safe, but they knew the outlaws had had no chance to spend any of it so they assumed it was all there in that tied-stack and in those pouches.

They also found something else. In the pockets of every one of those outlaws was a big wad of fresh currency. Cliff asked Sloat about that but by this time the captive's mouth was so purple-swollen the words made no sense when he tried to enunciate them.

Barney returned with the horses, the sun was high in the morning had finally turned off agreeably warm, right at the time when no one noticed.

Barney handed around the reins and said, "Riders comin' from the direction of town. But they're a hell of a long way south yet. Maybe Sam and a posse."

Cliff had mixed emotions about his brother-in-law's arrival up here. Sam was unpredictable at times, especially about something like this. Cliff nor Barney nor Jess were lawmen but they had certainly acted the part of lawmen.

On the other hand, Sam might be pleased at what had been accomplished. It had saved him a lot of saddle-backing and that was something he'd always liked—not having to ride too far nor work too long.

He rolled and lit a smoke, growled at Sloat to stand on his damned feet like a man, and turned to go over and kill a little time looking at the other prisoner.

He was young, no more perhaps than twenty years old. With a useless gun-hand his career as an outlaw was over even if he did not go down to Yuma Prison for being part of the robbery and murder in Centreville.

Cliff knelt and plugged the cigarette into the youth's gray lips. Evidently the pain was down to a solid dull ache because the young man nodded his head in appreciation, pulled back a big lungful, and let it out slowly. Whisky would have been a lot better, but the smoke helped and it was all there was.

NINE
The Woman

Sheriff Hart had five riders with him, all rangemen, which meant some cow outfit must have arrived in town a day or two early for their week-end blow-off. Or maybe the men riding up into the draw with Sam were itinerant riders he'd collected around town. When they were close enough to be seen adequately, neither Jess nor Cliff nor Barney knew a single one of them—just Sam Hart.

Cliff gestured, an unnecessary thing to do, Sam and his grave-faced possemen were already looking around where the fight had taken place.

Sam shook his head. "What did you have—a Gatling gun?"

He swung off and his brother-in-law said, "I want to borrow your horse, Sam."

The sheriff frowned. "What am I supposed to do—walk back?"

"Barney's coming with our animals. You ride my horse back." Cliff pointed. "One of them got away—the woman."

Sam stood a moment still scowling as he gazed over at Cliff. "It was them, eh? I saw the dude, but her . . ." Sam shook his head. He was by nature a gallant man; it just did not seem that women should be outlaws too. "Go ahead, take the horse. We'll see you in town. Hey Cliff—don't shoot her."

The lawman's animal was a big, rangy, pig-eyed bay with bones showing even though he was as fat as he would ever get. He was known throughout the township as one of the toughest using horses around.

Cliff walked him in the direction of the trees where he had last seen the woman, reins looped while he reloaded, then holstered, his six-gun.

The sun was high and there was enough heat between the low hills to the east and west to make a sort of dished out low cauldron of the meadow where Cliff was riding.

He felt the heat without heeding it. His attention was fixed dead ahead where the trees loomed closer by the moment.

She had no Winchester, of that he was certain, but inside that full, long skirt she could be concealing an entire small arsenal of handguns.

He had no trouble at all reading her sign for the first two hundred feet she had covered up through the trees. She had still been running. But after that he had a lot less to go on, and because he was not a very good tracker, he had to rely more or less on instinct and his knowledge of the countryside.

It was fifteen degrees cooler where tall old pine trees excluded sunshine except in a filtered way. It was also quiet, so he would not find her by noise she might be making.

He had two thing to rely upon. She was afoot, and therefore limited in how much ground she could cover, and she was most probably in country she was not at all familiar with.

The mountains lay on her left. That outlaw named Eb who had said something about riding into the mountains gave Cliff his idea of where to look. She was not dressed for it, but then she had not expected to have to trudge up into the mountains on foot, either.

He was following a game-trail and saw small boot-prints at a creek where someone had very recently knelt to drink. Encouraged by this he pressed along into the wilder back-country. Another time he found a thin piece of gray cloth where thorny bushes had snagged her skirt.

He was confident and unhurried. He simply did not want to ride right up onto her if she had a weapon, and he was satisfied that she would be armed one way or another. She would also no doubt hear him coming long before he saw her. That big bay horse had to make noise as he went along.

There were no scolding birds where he was riding. To an experienced hunter that would have been significant. Cliff was more interested in watching for additional sign of her passage.

Once, he heard cattle and that surprised him. No critters would normally come up this far; the grass was sparse and only in glades and parks. Also, this was bear and wolf and cougar country. Those scents would keep almost any other four-legged animal away.

But since he was not a cowman, nor concerned right at this time with livestock, he only briefly reflected upon what he had heard, and kept moving without haste but steadily. He had an animal under him which could easily outwalk the woman even with her head start.

There was a thin, long ridge on his left which he had hunted in autumns past and when he rode up it he heard the cattle again. This time he paused to look and listen. They were east of him but roughly parallel. He shook his head, looked elsewhere for movement south of him and ahead, saw nothing and waited a while, standing beside the rangy gelding.

Visibility was excellent from his point of vantage. Even so, he caught no sight of her. What he did see, however, was a thin stand of ancient dust up where pine-needles had been creating layers of dust and more crisp needles for centuries.

That would be the cattle.

He watched for a time, tried to guess who would be driving a little bunch of beef up in here, and very gradually began to suspect it was no one he'd know. In the first place this was Morgan-range, even most of the foothills and maybe as much as half the mountains. In the second place people did not herd cattle in the mountains; if they were going to drive them at all, they kept them *out* of forested country.

Rustlers.

It was a strong possibility and he was prepared to believe it, but he was still more concerned with finding that woman in the gray dress.

When he finally rode down off the rim, however, he proceeded with fresh caution.

The sun was high. In places, such as the creek-side

meandering thin long clearings, it was hot. He looked for more of her sign where the waterways ran but found no more places where she had tanked up.

Then his horse suddenly threw up its head, little ears forward, and Cliff stopped to look. The rustlers—if that's what they were—had either dropped down-slope a ways or Cliff had inadvertently angled higher than they were, but in either case his horse had probably detected the scent of other horses.

Cliff wished now that he had brought along one of those carbines from back yonder. Still in a forest, a man with a six-gun and plenty of trees around to step behind, was not entirely helpless.

He eased along another hundred or so yards, then left the horse tethered in shade and scouted onwards for about half a mile on foot.

He found the cattle. There were two rough-looking unshaven men driving them with the expertise of life-long rangemen. And they were preventing break-aways from sneaking through the trees to lower ground. The men clearly did not want their animals to reach open rangeland southward.

Cliff could not make out the pair of riders but he probably would not have known them anyway. This time of year all the cow outfits were hiring itinerant cowboys; men who had left their wintering places, usually in the south desert country, to ride north looking for work. A lot of those men never went to the same country two seasons in a row.

He advanced another hundred yards, far enough to

look for brands—and saw the big M on the sides of those fat redbacks. Mostly, they were young cows but there was also a sprinkling of steers among them.

One thing Cliff was reasonably certain of—none of Jess Turnbow's riders would have got over this far since last night, or early this morning, in their hunt for cattle. Moreover, these cattle were being driven *away* from Morgan-country, not towards it.

He speculated that these might be the animals Jess and his crew had been leisurely hunting yesterday, back through the brakes of the upper foothills.

He almost forgot his reason for being up here until a sixth sense told him he had not been very smart, leaving Sam's saddle horse back there unattended with that woman around here somewhere desperate for something to ride, so he went back. The horse was half asleep in his warm and pleasant shady place. There was no sign of anyone around—until just when Cliff was ready to walk the last twenty yards, then he saw the horse rouse up in interest, peering up the slope a distance, northward, and Cliff eased beside a big tree to also look up there.

He did not see her at once, not until she started moving again after apparently having halted in some particularly dark tree-shadows.

She was hatless now, her brown hair was down in disarray, she looked nearly exhausted and her skirt was torn in several places.

She had a six-gun in her right fist. It looked larger than it was because her hand was too small to adequately hold such a weapon. For some reason, Cliff had expected her to be armed with a belly-gun the way her brother had been armed.

He did not draw. There would be plenty of time for that, if it came down to that. He leaned and watched as she made slow, weary progress down the hill in the direction of Sam's bay gelding. She had just about used up whatever reserves of strength she'd started with. Her flight had been swift and prolonged across the canyon-meadow and for several hundred yards up through the forested slopes; he had read her sign that far. She had, he thought, run swiftly farther than he could have kept it up.

He had been interested in her back yonder and this curiosity re-appeared now as he watched her. She seemed to act as though the horse might have been deliberately left there, perhaps as bait, and this idea had never occurred to Cliff, nor, if it had, would he have tried anything that dangerous. If she got the horse, he would never see her again. He was sure of that. Moreover, it was his brother-in-law's prize possession.

The woman halted finally less than fifty yards away and the horse was gazing at her with particular interest, but with no evidence of fear or even uneasiness.

Cliff straightened up. He knew what *he* would do under these circumstances; when he got up close enough, he would come around to the horse's left side and snug up the cinch before untying the beast to mount it.

He also knew exactly what he would do if she did

that, so he waited, dappled over with camouflaging shade and diffused sunlight, motionless and intent.

She finally advanced until she was less than a hundred feet from the gelding, hung there poised for flight, head slowly turning left and right, six-gun hanging heavily at her side. Finally, she must have made up her mind to take the chance. She moved gracefully and soundlessly down to the horse, looked at him briefly, then did exactly what an experienced horseman would have done, she stepped around to the left side to lift the stirrup-leather and test the cinch. For this, she had to shove the six-gun into the waistband of her skirt.

Cliff did not see her do this but knew she had done it because he could see both her hands occupied with the latigo and cinch.

He quietly said, "Lady, don't touch that gun!"

She jumped back and started to whirl. That sudden startling movement made the horse swing in a shying motion. He bumped her and she went down in a flurry of gray cloth.

Cliff raised his Colt without cocking it although his thumb-pad was lightly atop the hammer.

He moved a little so she could locate him, and when she saw the gun as she curled to try and spring to her feet, she stopped moving, eyes widening as she stared upwards.

He went closer in a measured, slow walk, stopped and said, "Put your arms far out on both sides and lie still." He disarmed her, then straightened up to holster his Colt and offer a hand which she took and he drew up into a standing position. As they faced each other the distant bawling of those cattle came into the silence between them. She finally said, "My brother . . . ?"

"He made it through," Cliff told her. "You got any other weapons?"

While raising a hand to brush back waves of brown hair she shook her head. She was rather attractive but she was not pretty and probably never had been. Her features were too sharp and ferret-like, and her eyes, which were an unusual shade of pale blue and pale gray, showed almost no emotion at all—any time.

He did not trust her, but for them to get back in the direction of Centreville she would have to ride behind him on Sam's gelding. He thought he had the answer to that when he unloaded his Colt pocketed the slugs while she watched, then went over to untie the horse and swing up, kick free of the left stirrup and extend a hand.

She swung up easily. She was a sinewy woman, lean and evidently experienced and tough. She settled behind the cantle, long skirt at her knees, and held close by using his shellbelt, then she said, "I want to know what happened back there."

He told her as they rode, but because many of the details were unclear in his mind he only gave her a rough recounting. She did not make a sound as they angled towards the lower grassland. Even when they finally reached it, and were smitten at once by that high, hot sun, she said nothing.

Not until they were a mile southward angling westerly in the direction of town did she speak again. "What did my brother tell you?"

That was easy to answer. Cliff told her and for another distance she was quiet. Then she said, "He didn't knife that storekeeper."

"No? Who did?"

"One of the other men."

Cliff sighed. "Lady, none of those other men came to town. You and your brother rode out and met them after you'd killed the storekeeper and raided the safe. A friend and I tracked the whole band of you—then we backtracked you and your brother . . . One thing I don't know: Where did you get those horses you rode out of town on?"

She did not answer him.

They were about a third of the distance back when they saw riders approaching, a large band of them. She clung closer, clearly fearful, and when Cliff recognized Frank Morgan he reined off to make the interception.

Morgan and his bronzed riders looked with frank interest at the woman, but stocky Frank Morgan was a direct man. Whether he knew who she was or what she had been involved in, he was more interested in something else and Cliff anticipated it. He waved rearward with his right arm. "If it's stolen cattle, they are about four or five miles easterly up through the foothills into the timber. Two men are driving them."

Without a word Morgan bobbed his head then reined around and led his riders in a flinging rush towards the distant hills.

TEN
A Man And A Woman

For some length of time after they had encountered those bleak-faced rangemen with Frank Morgan the woman turned to look back occasionally. They had reached the north-south stageroad before she seemed reassured but then her interest turned towards the town which was not yet visible but which she knew was down there, and Cliff could sense her fresh concern.

He felt nothing about her one way or the other, except that she was a woman. Still, he offered a clumsy bit of comfort by saying, "They've never hung a woman yet, that I've heard about."

Her answer was terse. "There can be a first time."

He twisted to see her face. It was very close, the expression was equal parts exhaustion and fear which did not improve her attractiveness any. She said, "Watch ahead and don't get any ideas."

Cliff reddened, faced forward and had no more to say. They were within sight of rooftops when he felt her shift slightly behind him. At the same time he saw a freight wagon coming and called her attention to it. She leaned to make sure, straightened back and did not shift weight again.

He waited. Freight outfits were ponderous, the wagons heavy and high-sided. This rig had five teams in its hitch, all big Missouri-type mules. The animals alone were worth more than most freighters made in a year.

Cliff did not recognize the rig, but then he did not know them all anyway. When they were close enough, he did not know either the freighter on his high seat, nor the youthful, rather scrawny swamper. The men gazed impassively at those two people astride the same horse and the swamper leaned for a better look at the exposed female leg on the near side of Sam Hart's gelding. He leered.

The freighter was a large, burly, dark bearded man. He looked more like a swashbuckling pirate than a freight-hauler, and when they were abreast he nodded at Cliff, completely ignored Virginia Sloat, spat aside and whistled up his mules which had been instinctively preparing to halt, as though the big bearded man halted often when he met someone.

The rig was grinding dust into fine powder with its huge, wide rear steel tires. It was moving too slowly though to scuff the dust upwards.

Cliff rode impassively another hundred yards then abruptly halted and by curling his right leg around and over the saddlehorn, reached the ground with both reins in his hands.

The woman stared at him, with her brows beginning to sweep downwards and inwards.

He said, "Slide off, Miss Sloat."

She made no move to obey.

"Slide off or I'll pull you off!" He thought he knew what she was thinking and he was right. She said, "You lay a hand on me . . . !" and eased one set of fingers into the front of her dress.

He smiled. "That's what I want—that belly-gun."

It wasn't a derringer, it was a thin-bladed long stiletto beveled to sharpness on both sides of the blade. It had a silver-overlaid, filigreed handle. It was the most handsome dagger Cliff had ever seen. He gestured for her to throw it down. She delayed obeying until after she had said, "If you lay a hand on me I'll scratch your eyes out!"

He gestured again. "I'm not going to touch you unless you force me to. Now shuck that knife."

She let it drop. He retrieved it, studied it with interest, shoved it into his shellbelt and motioned again. "Get down."

"What for?" she demanded, apprehension in her eyes like unfurled flags.

"Because you're going to walk ahead of me from here. I wouldn't trust you if my life depended on it. Get down, and start hiking."

She did not offer a single objection as she swung off, settled her skirt and turned to walk past him. When she was thirty feet in front she turned her head. "What would it take for you to look the other way?"

"It wouldn't do you any good. Look around you; it's open country for miles in every direction. They could overtake you from town before you got halfway to the mountains."

"Not if you didn't tell them, cowboy." She smiled for the first time, but it was a calculating, assessing expression lacking warmth or even casual interest in him.

He pointed. "Walk!" Then he turned and sat waiting

for her to move. She looked steadily upwards for a long time, clearly organizing her thoughts and some additional words. He shook his head.

"You're wasting time. Walk or I'll nudge you along with the horse."

She said, "You bastard!" then turned and began walking, erect and with arms swinging, her anger so evident someone who might have been riding along would have been able to tell even from a distance how savage her mood was.

He rolled and lit a smoke. He was hungry but this might allay it for a short while. He saw no one after those freighters had passed, but occasionally he looked back, wondering about that pair of rustlers and the Morgan-riders.

He knew range-law as well as anyone else knew it. He also had a brother-in-law who was a lawman. He decided on a compromise; if Sam did not ask, he would not tell him anything. Maybe it was not an ethical compromise, but he believed in range-law as much as he believed in book-law. This was the first time he'd ever had to match them up, side by side, and it turned out not to be very hard. All he would do was—nothing. If Frank Morgan lynched a pair of rustlers, well, that was between Morgan and the rest of the world, it was neither Cliff Stanton's affair nor his concern.

He blew smoke, watched Virginia Sloat for a while, then glanced onward above her head where town roofs were visible as the hot sun began to turn a little cooler on its way over towards the westerly peaks.

It had been a long and arduous twenty-four hours. He missed the sleep but more than that he had a reaction to the action, and in this mood he said, "Miss Sloat; why does a woman become an outlaw?"

She walked, back still to him, and acted as though she were deaf.

He stopped her at the outskirts of town by riding up abreast, kicking out a boot and offering her his hand. She looked up, then shook her head to refuse his offer of allowing her to ride the rest of the way, lengthened her stride and headed down into town.

He pitied her. People turned to stare. She looked neither left nor right. Men tumbled from the saddleworks, the gunshop, the saloon, to stare and to make little comments aside while grinning and snickering. Cliff reddened.

Sam came from his jailhouse office, shoved back his hat and stood, thumbs hooked in his shellbelt, gazing northward. When she got close he jerked his head. Without a word passing between them she marched over and halted in overhang shade out front of the jailhouse, her face shiny, her blue-gray emotionless eyes moving slowly back and forth among the onlookers, her lips pressed flat in an ugly look of defiance.

Sam waited until Cliff had dismounted, then looked the horse over before saying, "She had that knife?"

Cliff handed it over. "She may have a belly-gun, I didn't search her. Anyway; be careful of her, Sam."

The lawman nodded, then said, "A rider come for Jess. He split out of here like he'd been shot out of a cannon."

Cliff's gaze did not waver. "Is that so? What about the others?"

"We caught their loose-stock and lashed them aboard to fetch them back. Incidentally, there are a pair of damned mad cowboys over at Sandal's saloon. Someone stole their saddle animals right out of their camp last night."

Cliff now knew where the Sloats had got those two horses they had escaped on after the killing and robbery. "So you got 'em on a charge of horse-stealin' too."

Sam brushed that aside. "Martin's killin' comes first. Don't tell anyone it was Sloat who did it."

"I won't. How about Barney?"

"He give me his word." Sam glanced up the roadway. "He's got something to tell about for the rest of his life, and he's up there right now making it taller and taller. Like he did it single-handed, or I don't know Barney Sandal."

Cliff almost said that in fact Barney had done most of the accurate shooting up there; he decided not to. That affair was one of those things it was better to just try and forget.

"I'll take your horse down to the barn and stable him. Thanks for his use, Sam."

"All right. Then you want to come back and listen in when I talk to those folks?"

Sam smiled tiredly. "What I want is some food, a bath, and some sleep. They're your headache from here on."

He trudged down the roadway to Hanson's place, handed Saul the reins with orders. "Grain, flaky green hay, a damned good cuffing, and later on, water."

Saul waited, then said, "You catch her?"

"Yeah." Cliff turned before the next question was asked and started up the roadway. He got as far as the little crooked alleyway leading to Mex-town and that very handsome liquid-eyed Mexican woman stepped out.

"Are you tired?" she asked. Then she said, "Alfonso wants to talk to you."

He smiled at her. Tiredness was something which could be postponed. She turned and led the way.

ELEVEN
Another Day

Alfonso had shaved and looked as though he might also have bathed and changed his britches and shirt, but he still retained that unkempt look of men who lived alone.

The pretty Mexican woman did not enter. She stood aside for Cliff to duck in through the doorway. It was blessedly cool in the Gutierrez *jacal*.

Alfonso gazed enquiringly, then went to a cupboard for twin cups and a bottle of wine which he placed upon the table between them as he said, "You interested in knowing who came over here to tell me who had killed Martin Hamm?"

Cliff was too tired to guess. "Who?"

"Barney Sandal."

Cliff tasted the wine. It was warm, but it was smooth and fragrant. He could feel it gently reviving him all the way down. He smiled at Gutierrez. "His way of apologizing, I guess."

Alfonso reached for his cup. "I guess. They told us you'd gone after the woman."

"I got her. She's over at the jailhouse. That ought to end it. Unless someone starts more lynch-talk."

Gutierrez doubted that would happen. Not with Sam Hart in town. "Who killed Martin?"

Cliff sipped more tepid wine. "Sam asked me not to say."

Alfonso studied his friend for a moment. "The man and the woman. It's not hard to figure out—if you saw their tracks coming alone out of town."

"Well, it'd be better if folks didn't know, just in case someone does start hangrope talk again . . . Al, how's your back?"

Gutierrez suddenly reddened and drank wine for a moment before putting down the cup to avoid Cliff's gaze. "It is much better. A friend helped me with it. Much better."

Cliff kept gazing across the table. "Same friend that made you clean up and shave and change your duds?"

Alfonso smiled. "Same one."

Cliff arose, drained his cup, felt the effect almost instantly and said, "I'm hungry as a bitch wolf." At the door he looked back. "Marry her, Al. She's as pretty as a palomino colt."

He trudged back up through the crooked alleyway, and turned toward the cafe before the full force of an empty stomach and that wine overtook him. He had to cover the last hundred feet by slitting his eyes, selecting a target, which was the cafe doorway, and measuring his steps with care. Otherwise he would have staggered, and by the time he got up there, it was not one door it was two of them.

The cafeman slanted a knowing glance and word-lessly shoved hot black coffee in front of Cliff, then also without speaking went back to his cooking area to fetch Cliff a plate of steak and potatoes with apple sauce and baking-flour biscuits. Then he brought all this back, shoved it in front of Cliff and settled ample hips against the pie-table at his back and sucked his teeth while watching his only customer eat.

After a while he said, "You done a good lick of work, Cliff. Sam was in a while ago. Yes, sir, you done a good lick of work."

Cliff went on eating. The coffee helped so he had another cup then he went right on eating. The cafeman finally had to go prepare something for a stage-driver named Kelley who had just come in tugging off gauntlets, instead of gloves, the badge of his calling, although as a matter of fact a lot of drivers had stopped wearing that ostentatious, Buffalo Bill kind of glove long ago. Kelley sank down, tipped back his hat, looked at the cafeman until he had ordered, then turned slightly as he recognized Cliff Stanton.

Kelley was a hearty, likable man, thick-shouldered,

scarred, with a blue bold gaze. He said, "Wish you'd been herdin' my rig tonight when I came down through." He waited for Cliff to evince interest. Cliff was sobering up, and was purely occupied with this, so he did not even look at Kelley.

The whip was not offended. He had known Cliff Stanton fifteen years and had in fact ridden his first coach on the high-seat with Cliff as his boss and instructor.

"There was a couple of fellers dangling from oaks right beside the damned road."

Cliff's fork stopped mid-way. "Whereabouts?"

"Six, eight miles northward. Up there on Morgan-range."

"Tonight?"

"Yeah, and if they hadn't been hung right next to the road we wouldn't have seen 'em. There ain't a moon. Whoever draped them like that, broke necks with the ropes still around 'em, did it on purpose to scare off other fellers. By gawd it liked to scairt me off, and I didn't do anything wrong."

The cafeman shuffled forth listening with interest. "You recognize 'em?" he asked Kelley. The stager shook his head. "Didn't try'n recognize them, Will. Didn't stop an' cut them down neither. I cussed up the hitch and flogged it all the way to town."

The roadway door opened. Neither Cliff nor Kelley paid any attention but the cafeman looked over their heads as he said, "Howdy, Sheriff."

Cliff looked. Sam beckoned. "Finish your supper," he said. "I'll wait out here."

Cliff was finished, all but a couple of mouthfuls. He tossed down some silver and went out front into the warm darkness. Sam offered no preliminaries. "Was Kelley telling you about a couple of hung fellers up near the foothills?"

Cliff nodded.

"Well come along. I got a wagon up the road. We'll go cut them down and fetch them back."

Cliff shook his head. "This time go do your own dirty work. I'm wore down to a nibbling." He turned and walked in the direction of his small house and for once its emptiness when he entered to light a lamp did not bother him. At least not as much as it had been bothering him since last autumn, but there was a loneliness and a chill which would not have been evident if his wife had still been alive.

He slept like a dead man and did not even stir until sunrise, which was unusual for him. As he arose he attributed this to Al Gutierrez's red wine, to eating all that heavy food at Will's cafe, to having been without rest for an unaccustomed long time over the previous couple of days, and finally to the fact that he had not been twenty-five years old now for twenty years.

Sam arrived as Cliff was making breakfast. Sam looked, then said, "You just got up?"

Cliff grinned self-consciously, pointed to a chair and gave his brother-in-law the first cup of coffee from the new batch he had just brewed. Sam smacked his lips. "Fair java," he announced, then watched Cliff for a moment before saying, "I got those two fellers someone hung and put them in back of the icehouse, Cliff."

Stanton slid several leaden pancakes onto a plate and turned down the stove-damper, all with his back to the sheriff. "Did you?"

Sam drank more coffee. "Yeah. Cliff, when you rode northeast after that woman, did you know Jess Turnbow and the riders with him you and Barney met up yonder was lookin' for some Big M cattle that had been lost?"

Cliff sat down with his plate. Sam knew the answer to that question. He had ridden back to town with Jess, they had talked. Sam probably suspected what Cliff knew and was probing for that now, too.

But the moment he admitted one thing to his brother-in-law he was going to have to admit all the rest of it too. He started to eat. "Yeah, something was said about cattle."

Sam finished his coffee and arose to go to the stove to refill the cup. "And when you found that woman . . . who else did you see up yonder?"

Cliff put down his knife and fork. "Sam, if you got something to say, just spit it out. Damn it."

Sheriff Hart turned, over at the stove. "Did you meet Frank Morgan up there, maybe with some of his riders?"

"What if I did?"

"As sure as I'm standing here, Frank hanged those two fellers."

"How do you know that, Sam?"

"Because I got handbills on those two. One was named Hollander and the other one was named Cleve, and they got long records down along the border country as rustlers. And if those two were in the foothills, and Big M was missing some cattle . . ." Sam sampled his coffee and returned to the table with it. "Frank Morgan may be the biggest wheel in Morgan Valley but he can't break the law any more than anyone else can."

Cliff tried another couple of mouthfuls then put down the knife and fork again, reaching for his cup of coffee. "You need a witness to pin Frank to the hangings, is that it, Sam?"

Hart nodded.

"You'll have to look somewhere else." Cliff drank half the coffee before speaking again. "I saw Frank up there. Him and some of his riders. But I didn't see them hang anyone and I didn't see them hunt down rustlers. I didn't even see them head into the hills. I had that woman behind the saddle with me and I wanted to get back here to town with her. Sam; that's all I know."

He sat waiting for the question he feared—had he encountered those two rustlers?—but all his brother-in-law said was: "Then I'll have to get it from the men who were with Frank Morgan."

Cliff waited a moment to say, "You'll play hell, Sam. No one's going to tell you anything that might get them arrested as accomplices."

"If I arrest them *first* they might. I've used that trick before. Arrest one man, make a trade with him, his freedom for a sworn affidavit. It works, Cliff." Sam did not lower his eyes. His gaze was steely and speculative. "How many times we been on opposite sides of the fence, Cliff? Damned few times in twenty years. Never anything serious."

"You're sure we're on opposite sides this time, Sam?"

Sheriff Hart nodded his head. "I've heard you say a hundred times that range-law is good law."

"It is good law."

Sheriff Hart did not even reply to that. He toyed with his coffee cup for a while in thought. When he eventually arose he said, "I sent a couple of tame In'ians up through there this morning to read the sign and tell me what happened."

Cliff's heart sank a little, but he had an answer to that. "Can you hang a man on the say-so of some trackers who weren't even up there yesterday?"

Sheriff Hart thinly smiled. "I expect not, but it'll be good enough to use on some dumb damned rangerider who was with Morgan yesterday."

They went to the door together. Cliff and Sam Hart had always been close friends, even before Cliff had married Sam's sister. It troubled Stanton now that he could see how things were progressing between them. As Sam stepped out upon the little front porch Cliff said, "Sam, you got two outlaws in the icehouse and it's over for them. Hangin' men like that's been the cow-country custom since we were kids. It makes sure at least those two won't steal any more cattle, or horses, or maybe kill any more people. Don't tell me you can't look the other way. I've seen you do it on other occasions."

"But not murder," replied the sheriff, and this of course was the crux of the matter. Frontier cattlemen had never considered that variety of extermination murder, they had considered it justifiable execution. There were very few old-time rangemen who had not at one time or another leaned upon a hangrope, yet they still obeyed the law, went to church, raised law-abiding families and were respectable members of their communities.

Sam stood waiting for Cliff to make the obvious protest, but Cliff did not say it. He said something different. "Give it time. Let it go for a few weeks, Sam."

"How do I do that? I got those damned outlaws in the icehouse and we got to have a burial and folks already suspect something. You can't just ride into town with a couple of fellers dead in a wagon with rope-marks around their gullets and not have folks start talking." Sheriff Hart turned to gaze briefly up and down the morning-bright roadway, then turned back to also say, "And Frank Morgan knows better than to do something like that. His paw and grandpaw got away with it because there was no law in Morgan Valley those days. But Frank . . ." Sam shook his head, turned and walked away.

Cliff went back to finish breakfast but his appetite was gone so he put the leftovers in a tin dish on the rear porch. In Centreville there was no garbage disposal, but there usually did not have to be. Before nightfall that tin dish out there would be licked to shiny emptiness; dogs around town had regular routes day to day.

Cliff went down to the liverybarn to make certain Saul had taken care of the horse Sam Hart had ridden back to town yesterday, and encountered old Lew Calkins the saddlemaker.

Lew had originally arrived in Morgan Valley when it had one of those tongue-twisting Indian names. He had come in behind one of the last drives Frank Morgan's grandfather had brought to the country. Old Lew had known them all, not just Frank's grandfather, but his father as well, and almost all the old-time riding-hands which had served Big M. He had also known all the other old-timers around Morgan Valley. He was one of the small handful of those men still above ground, and he was forever predicting that he was just barely being able to keep out of a six-foot hole himself, except that this morning he and Saul had drunk some Irish coffee in the harness-room so when Lew met Cliff Stanton out front in the warm shade of a big old unkempt cottonwood tree, Lew was feeling in fine condition. He even joked a little about Cliff riding all the way back to town with that woman behind his saddle. And he salaciously winked about that.

Only when Cliff mentioned the pair of hanged rustlers did old Lew's expression undergo a change; it settled into deep lines of solid approval of what had happened. "Hang 'em once," he pronounced, using the old-time cowman axiom, "and you never have to do it again, and you clean up the world a little bit."

Cliff said, "Ever try convincing my brother-in-law of that?"

Lew hadn't. "No, but that don't change nothing. Them two are dead aren't they?"

"Yeah, and Sam's going after Frank Morgan for hanging them."

"Can he prove Frank done it?"

"Sam's no fool, Lew. He's got ways."

The old man pondered a moment before letting go with a rattling big sigh. "Change ain't always for the best, Cliff. In fact the older I get the more I figure maybe it's not the best maybe about half the time. Well; I got to get up to the shop and do some work. Much as I like bein' out in this sunshine and all . . ." He went shuffling northward up the plankwalk, head low in thought, lined, wrinkled old face set in its craggy and customary solemn expression of half-anxiety, half-disapproval.

Saul Hanson came out and invited Cliff into the harness-room. Evidently Saul had made several trips because his face was slightly flushed, his eyes were bright, and he was wearing a fixed, vacuous smile, and hell, it wasn't even nine o'clock in the morning.

Cliff declined. He got just about all the whisky-boost he'd need for the balance of this day just from Saul's breath.

He went looking for his horse, found the animal contentedly eating meadow hay in a corral out back. He had been curried and grained and watered, and looked as though he hadn't been ridden recently until his tail dragged. He was a young animal; they recovered more quickly than older horses.

TWELVE
Sheriff Hart's Scheme

Barney Sandal did not show up at the saloon all that day. When he should have gone home last night because of his condition of exhaustion he had instead fortified himself with whisky and, being the center of attraction for townsmen and rangeriders alike, he had done exactly what Sheriff Hart had predicted, he had harangued his patrons until almost one o'clock in the morning when he began to run down like an old clock.

This morning, when Cliff had been talking to the saddlemaker, Barney had been at home sick as a dog and in bed. It had also been a long while since Barney had been twenty-five.

Sam Hart was fresh enough, but then he had not even left town until the fighting was just about finished, and Sam had been sleeping through each night for weeks.

Cliff needed some baking powder, some flour and coffee at the store but because for some reason he did not want to enter the place, he therefore went back home without buying anything, and he was still there later, when the wispy, nervous individual who was area supervisor for the Greenwood Stage Company, Amos Shepler, came over to see if he might inveigle Cliff into taking a night-run southward because his regular whip was down on his back in the corralyard bunkhouse with a bad case of the grippe.

Cliff knew Amos Shepler, had worked for him over the years. He cocked an eye and said, "You got other substitute whips, Amos."

"Yeah, but not around Centreville, Cliff, and I'd take it as a personal favor if you'd do this for me just this once. You only got to drive down as far as Preston, lie over, and ride back on the northbound in the morning. After that, I'll have a new feller here. He's already on his way from Cheyenne. Clifford, just this once."

Cliff nodded. "But just this one time. I'm out of that business. Don't expect to ever get back into it, even on a substitute basis. By the way, Amos, did they bring in that mud-wagon from southeasterly along a little creek where it was abandoned?"

Shepler brightened. "Sure did. Saul's lads taken a hitch down and drove it back for Sam. It's over in the corralyard now. It come from some place in Montana called Monument. It was stole up there and hid by some outlaws. Sam was telling me about it." Amos wrinkled his nose like a nervous little wiry rabbit and departed leaving Cliff to start an early supper. He was not particularly hungry but when Sam walked in just ahead of sundown he invited his brother-in-law to stay and Sam, whose meals came from Will's cafe, agreed. He looked in the pans atop the stove, but he still agreed. In fact, Sam would have stayed for supper if Cliff had been baking dog. The cafeman's food was usable, no one had died of it that folks had heard about, but his main ingredient in anything—steaks, spuds, even pies and cakes—was grease.

He was telling Cliff this—for the thousandth time over the past twenty years—when he suddenly also said, "And those trackers I sent out this morning got back about an hour ago."

Cliff had not believed Sam had come along just to beat him out of a supper. "Is that a fact?"

"They made a fair reconstruction of everything up there. Odd thing how In'ians still put a lot of faith in that old-time stuff."

Cliff stoked the firebox with fresh sticks of wood and opened the damper wide. "You know, Sam, whenever you get into one of these clever moods of yours, your voice changes; it gets sort of schemin' and quiet." Cliff turned. "Just say it right out."

Sam was agreeable. "Did you know that my bay horse got astraddle a chunk of wagon-tire last spring and I've had to have him shod with a spreader on his right front foot ever since, because he cut himself pretty bad around the pastern and one back quarter?"

"No, I didn't know that. And what's it got to do with what we're talking about?"

"Those Indian boys picked up the sign of that spreader-shoe . . . Cliff, you told me you never saw those rustlers."

"I never told you any such a thing, Sam. I told you I saw Frank Morgan and some men with him, but you never asked if I'd seen anyone else."

Sam Hart was not annoyed. His eyes bored in as he said, "You saw those rustlers, Cliff."

"I saw two men driving cattle, is what I saw, Sam, and I was looking for that woman. I never got close enough to see the faces of those men. I couldn't even tell you from lookin' at 'em now over in the icehouse if it was the same pair. I didn't pay any attention to what they were wearing. Like I said—"

"Yeah. You was lookin' for the woman." Sheriff Hart sighed and sat down pushing thick legs far out so he could study his scuffed boot-toes. "But you saw two men driving Big M beef easterly off Big M range, and you knew from what Jess told you they were missing some cattle." Sam suddenly looked up. "Cliff, I know you pretty well. You didn't see men driving off Big M cattle without at least wondering why they'd be going east, and why they was driving cattle through the foothills instead of out in the open. You figured they was rustlers, Cliff."

For a while no more was said. The two iron fry-pans on the stove, one with slabs of steak-meat, the other with hoe-cake potatoes, seemed to occupy all Cliff's attention.

Sam sat over there relaxed and comfortable, and hungry. He brought forth a plug and considered gnawing off a corner, then decided not to and repocketed the thing. It was just as well, he would have had to step discreetly to the back door and spit out his cud because shortly afterwards Cliff heaped two plates, filled two coffee cups, and put those things upon the

113

table. As he sat down he said, "If those outlaws stole that mud-wagon up in Montana and robbed someone up there, how's it come a posse didn't overtake them?"

Sam dropped his hat to the floor beside his seat and reached for the knife and fork. He was perfectly willing to discuss this other matter, but anyone who knew Sam Hart would have known he had never for a moment given up on what he had been discussing before the mud-wagon was brought up.

"They didn't use the mud-wagon right away," he explained. "They had it hid about fifty miles south of the place where they made their robbery. Between the town of Monument and the wagon, they made off on horses they had also stole up there. The posse followed horse-tracks—naturally."

Cliff understood. "When they ran out of horse-tracks they turned back?"

Sam nodded while vigorously chewing stringy beef. "And later on when folks saw a mud-wagon with passengers inside, even a lady in a gray dress and all, they never associated it with the robbery at Monument." Sam swallowed, drank some coffee and said, "What the hell did this critter die of—being run to death?"

Cliff ignored that. "Did you find some money on those outlaws after the fight in the arroyo?"

"Yeah," replied Sam, trying to dislodge a piece of boot-sole steak with more coffee. "I don't know yet how much they raided up at Monument; just wrote the letter this morning. But when they answer I'll know. But hell, it won't all be there."

"Ask the Sloats."

Sheriff Hart put a pained look upon his brother-in-law. "What do you think I been doing? They quit talking last night. Won't even give me the time of day any more."

Sam finally got the piece of steak down his gullet. "Cliff—this is a terrible piece of meat."

When his host made no comment, nor made any apology, Sheriff Hart went back to work on the steak. "I want to explain something to you," he said, his tone changing slightly. "You know enough about how the law works to understand that by withholding evidence from me—"

"Sam, damn it, I told you everything I saw up there. Every blessed thing."

Hart smiled humorlessly. "I hope you did, because I'm going out first thing in the morning and bring in Frank Morgan. And he'll fight this thing down to the last scrap of bone. Which means I'll have to dragoon every witness I got."

Cliff scowled. "What witnesses?"

"You, mainly."

"And who else—what does 'mainly' mean?"

Sam chewed, and chewed, and chewed, then stretched his neck when he swallowed, and afterwards gave it up, putting aside his utensils to reach for the coffee cup. It was empty so he went to the stove for a refill.

Cliff persevered. "What does 'mainly' mean?"

"Those In'ians who read all the sign," replied Sheriff

Hart returning to the table. "This is one night I should have eaten at the cafe."

Cliff let his supper guest return to his chair before saying, "A couple of darned Indian trackers—Sam—you don't expect that to convince a court do you? With Frank Morgan and his lawyer on the other side?"

The sheriff's answer was almost detached in its dispassionate pronouncement. "I'm not trying to hang Frank Morgan. Personally, I wish to hell he had been back east. But he sure as hell lynched those rustlers and my job is to make the best case I can to prove it. I got to do what I can."

Cliff was not fooled one bit by this disclaimer. "You never went half-hog after anything in your life, Sam. You're going to hang Morgan if you can."

Sheriff Hart would not be drawn into this kind of personal dispute. He began eating the potatoes and did not bother that piece of indigestible steak again. When the meal was finished he said, "You're going to die young, eating stuff like this."

He brought forth his plug, nestled a cud into his cheek and leaned back in the chair studying Cliff. "Alfonso Gutierrez is going to marry old Sanchez's daughter. Did you know that?"

Cliff hadn't *known* it but he'd been encouraging the idea so he was not surprised. "She's as pretty as a dawn sky," he remarked and his brother-in-law solemnly inclined his head. "And you?"

Cliff blinked. "Me—what? Get married?"

"Yeah. And I know what you're thinking. She was

my sister. Cliff; she's plumb gone. Somewhere, she's happy—I hope with all my heart. But you keep on eatin' like you are now and you aren't goin' to make it through many more winters."

Cliff was reaching for his makings when a thought occurred to him. Sam Hart was not particularly a devious man, but he was a lot more clever than most folks gave him credit for being. Nor was Cliff baited away from the main theme of their supper-table talk by Sam's concern for his welfare and his eating habits.

He lit up, blew smoke, fixed Sam with a hard look and said, "Those other witnesses—you aren't going out there in the morning just to arrest Morgan, are you?"

"I already told you—I'm going to figure out which of his riders has got a weak chin, then I'm going to arrest that feller too. And if that one don't spill the beans, then I'll arrest another one; maybe the whole blessed passle of them. I'll get witnesses, Cliff, you can bet your boots on that."

For a while they sat regarding one another, then Sam struggled up to his feet. He said he still had to make his round of the town before heading for Barney's place for his nightly slug of rye whisky.

After he departed, Cliff sat a while alone, at the supper table, finished his smoke and began cleaning up.

Whatever the outcome of those hangings was, he was certainly in the clear. But when he testified that he had met Morgan and his riders, and told them where their cattle were, he would certainly be placing Frank

Morgan—and his cowboys—in a bad position. Circumstantial evidence or not, a lot of cemeteries beyond a lot of cowtowns had a lot of men in them committed to the soil on no better evidence. Cowcountry judges, and juries, had plenty of unspoken bias against lynching. Especially if they came from the towns rather than the ranges.

Frank Morgan would never speak to Cliff Stanton again, even if he were acquitted.

That did not necessarily cause Cliff to lose any sleep. He and Frank Morgan had never more than nodded to one another anyway. But it stuck in Cliff's craw to have men perhaps sent to prison for something he was not entirely unsympathetic to.

He bedded down with a loud sigh. When that affair of Martin Hamm's killing and the safe robbery had been concluded he had been certain life around Centreville would return to normal. Now it wouldn't, and he was again being hauled into something he wanted no part of.

He slept without troubled thoughts, however. He almost never slept any other way.

In the morning he had finished making breakfast and cleaning up before he went outside to dole out the contribution to the local curs in his back-porch tin dish. He heard horsemen riding up through town and stepped around the side of the house.

It was his brother-in-law with four possemen. Cliff shook his head. If Sam was going to brace Frank Morgan, who had at least seven steady riders working for him this season, Sam should have taken more than just four men, if he expected trouble, and Morgan was known as a man with a temper and a strong will.

Well, that was Sam's problem. Cliff returned to the house to do some house-cleaning, something at which he had never been adept and towards which he had always held a private conviction which was not charitable towards wives, or ladies who came in once a week to dung out after bachelors.

He had avoided hiring one of those local ladies up until now, but as he worked away the morning the idea kept recurring to him that he was not by build nor temperament good at what he was trying to do, so maybe after all it might be a good idea to hire one of those ladies. He would not have to be there when she went at it.

His main, deep-down feeling about this until now had been based upon some idea that he did not want any other woman in the house he and his wife had shared so pleasantly for so many years.

But, as Sam kept saying, his wife was gone, and life, he knew for a fact, kept right on going.

THIRTEEN
An Angry Man

Al Gutierrez walked up through the back-alley to Cliff's house while the day was still fresh, the sun new, and the morning only beginning to get warm.

He had with him some freshly-made *chorrizo,* a present from the old man named Sanchez who had years earlier worked with Lew Calkins in the harness shop. No one made *chorrizo* like old Sanchez. Not everyone ate it, especially in *gringo*-town, despite the assurance of most Mexicans that it prevented worms and killed the ones which a person might have an infestation of.

According to Will over at the cafe, who never served it, *chorrizo* would also kill people, if they ate it long enough, which clearly was untrue; Mex-town had a lot of very old people in it who had been eating *chorrizo* all their lives.

Cliff liked it, but then he had been instructed meticulously in how to prepare it before eating it, which made all the difference. If a person did not first boil it until most of the red grease was cooked out, before broiling it, *chorrizo* was a very hot—usually too hot for *gringo* gullets—sausage made of—hopefully—clean beef and red peppers.

Cliff had liked it the first time he had eaten it. When Alfonso handed him the greasy package Cliff grinned and thanked his friend, then they sat for a cup of java in the clean kitchen because clearly Alfonso had something else on his mind.

They discussed the Sloats, the fight up in the canyon, Sam's earlier departure from town, the matter of those hanged rustlers even the possibilities of a late springtime rain to "set" range-grass and keep the creeks running, before Alfonso finally said, "Cliff, are you a Catholic?"

Stanton blinked. He wasn't an "anything," hadn't

been inside a church since last autumn when a friend died and before that it had been longer than he could recall. He shook his head. "Why?"

"I'm going to marry her. I want you to stand up for me."

Cliff smiled. "If you didn't marry her I was fixing to ask her myself. I'll be right proud to be your best man, Al." He leaned and offered a hand. They shook then Cliff raised his cup of coffee. "To a long life full of many boy-children, fast horses and good whisky, Al."

Gutierrez nervously laughed and returned the toast. "I got a job," he announced, and shrugged. "Well; a man can make out by himself, but with a wife he has to look ahead. No?"

"Yeah, he does for a fact. Where is the job?"

"Calkins' shop. I worked with her father last winter with leather. He taught me a little about harness and saddlery. Old Calkins asked me, so I hired on. I think her father went to Calkins when she told him we would be married." Al considered his cup. "It's a good trade. People will always need saddles and harness. Nothing can take the place of horses."

Cliff would have agreed with that but someone banged on his front door with an iron fist so he arose to go see who it was.

Frank Morgan was standing out there, alone. Cliff was surprised enough to just stare until Morgan said, "We're going to talk," then Cliff stepped aside for the cowman to enter. But he was mystified; if Morgan was here in town he had to have left his ranch hours earlier, which meant Sam had missed him, and would not find him at the ranch. That added another dimension to Cliff's bewilderment. If Morgan did not know Sam was after him with a posse, then he wouldn't know that Cliff had helped send the sheriff to the ranch.

He said, "You like a cup of coffee?"

Morgan, a compact, square-jawed man in his late forties, shook his head. "No. I want to tell you that going about it as underhandedly as you did, scaring off my riders, puts you in a damned bad situation with me."

Cliff began a slow scowl. "What are you talking about, Mister Morgan?"

The cowman's lips flattened. "Don't get cute with me, Stanton."

Cliff's temper rose a notch. "I'm not being cute with you. I don't have any idea what you're talking about. But if you came here this morning for trouble, I'll do my best to oblige you. . . . Scairt off your riders?"

"You sneaked out to the ranch last night and told them the law was coming after me and my riders this morning for hanging two rustlers!"

"I didn't do any such a damned thing, Mister Morgan. I haven't even been on your range since I saw you when I was bringing back that woman yesterday. Last night I was right here at home—all the damned night. In fact, my brother-in-law had supper with me and after he left I went to bed." Cliff paused to study the square, bronzed face of the cowman for a moment. "How could anyone scare off your riders?"

"I just told you; by warning them the law was going

to try and get them sent to prison for those hangings!"

Cliff slowly shook his head. "I haven't even seen any of your men since the fight in the canyon, and then it was only Jess Turnbow . . . Mister Morgan? That's the gospel truth."

Frank Morgan was a good judge of men. He shifted position from one foot to the other foot, a grudging doubt firming up in his mind. Before he could speak, Cliff said, "But Sam did ride out of town this morning with a posse to arrest you. I saw him heading out. And last night at supper he told me he was going to do that . . . And in case you'd like to know, I been disagreeing with him about those hangings. Like they say, Mister Morgan, when folks hang rustlers that's one pair that won't ever steal another cow, or horse, or maybe shoot any more people."

Morgan looked down, tugged at one glove, then at the other glove. While occupied at this he gruffly said, "Who the hell did go out there in the dark last night and talk to my boys in the bunkhouse? This morning they were all gone. Just Jess was still around."

"He'd ought to know, hadn't he?"

"No. He's got quarters off the back of the bunkhouse, to himself. He didn't hear a thing. This morning their bedrolls, saddles, horses, everything they owned was gone. He was just as surprised as I was." Morgan looked up.

Cliff's astonishment was too genuine to be acting. Morgan glanced around the room and back again. "*Someone* from town rode out there and scairt them off.

You knew we'd gone after the cattle and those rustlers. No one else knew it."

Cliff thought back. It hit him like a blow between the eyes. *Old Lew Calkins!* The more he dwelt on this possibility the more he could confirm his suspicions. Not only had he told Calkins, but the old man, who belonged to that older generation which believed wholeheartedly in justifiable execution, had made remarks which had left no doubt of his view of the matter.

"Hell," he said, and returned Morgan's gaze.

"Who?" the cowman demanded.

Cliff did not answer, but he said, "Someone did you a hell of a favor, Mister Morgan. Sheriff Hart can't nail you to the fence without witnesses. He knows it too. Someone else figured that out and did you a favor. Sam was going to bring in some of your riders too, for his witnesses. By yourself, with no one to say they even saw you catch those men, let alone hang them, a lawyer can get it thrown out. I'll bet a new pair of boots on that."

Morgan's broad, low forehead got two creases across it as he stood staring at Cliff Stanton. He tugged at his gloves again, and after a long silence he raised his head.

"I thought it was some kind of trick someone was playing who doesn't like me; scaring off my riders at the height of the riding season."

"I don't know whether someone didn't like you or not, Mister Morgan, but they sure as hell didn't believe anyone should be punished for hanging rustlers. Lots of folks would feel that way."

"You, Stanton?"

"Leave me out of it," retorted Cliff. "If I was you, I'd go on down to Sam's office and be sitting there when he comes back to town. From my experience, Mister Morgan, it seems to me the best way to win a fight is to hit first and never let the other feller get his guard up . . . And Sam's going to be hopping mad when he gets back, after discovering all his witnesses are gone."

Frank Morgan cleared his throat. "About that coffee. . . ."

Cliff stepped past and opened the door. "I'm fresh out," he said, and stood until the cowman had walked back to the front porch, then Cliff said, "You never impressed me as a feller who'd go off half-cocked." He closed the door and went back to the kitchen where Al Gutierrez was sitting with wide eyes. Cliff got another cup of coffee from the stove, still angry.

"I should have punched him in the nose," he mumbled, returning to the table. As he sat down he glanced over at Gutierrez. Al shrugged heavy shoulders.

Later, Cliff walked over to the harness works. Old Calkins was straddling a sewing-horse stitching a pair of leather harness traces. He looked up, nodded and went back to work.

Cliff pulled up a horseshoe-keg, sat down and said, "Where's that old Texas A-fork saddle you ride, Lew?"

Calkins went on stitching for a moment, then slowly put aside his awl and let the threaded needles dangle as he put an expressionless gaze upon the younger man. "Why do you want to know, Cliff?"

"Because, darn you, Frank Morgan was just over at my place mad as a wet hen because he thought it was me snuck out there last night and scairt his riders out of the country."

Old Calkins wiped his hands upon the faded apron he wore, then studied the worn, blunt fingers as he said, "What riders?"

Cliff threw up his hands. "You damned well know what riders. Yesterday when we talked out front of the liverybarn , . . Lew; I'm not going to say anything about it, but if Sam ever finds out he'll skin you alive."

"If you don't never say anything, how's he going to find out?"

"From some of those riders."

Calkins slowly wagged his head. "They never even looked back. I sat out there for two hours in the dark, watching them slip out, saddle up without a sound and hit the trail. They'll never be back in Morgan Valley. Cliff . . . Do I look like a fool? I figured that before I got out there. I made it one hell of a story, and it was true; they could go to prison for life. And you know it. And they knew it too, when I got through tellin' them Sheriff Hart was coming with a posse."

Cliff studied the parchment-like old face with its steady, tough eyes. "Where's the old Texas saddle, Lew?"

"Out back. Why?"

"Because I haven't seen you on a horse in ten years,

and neither has anyone else." Cliff arose off the little keg. "Sam's no fool. He might figure something out. I don't know how, but he might. So if I was in your boots, I'd go sift some dirt and dust over that saddle so it won't look like it's been ridden."

The saddlemaker nodded his head. "All right . . . It's a good thought at that. As for riding out—Cliff, when you're my age horse-backing is hard and it's painful in every stiff joint you got."

"But you went anyway."

Calkins did not waver. "When a man believes in things, he's got a responsibility to them, hasn't he?"

Cliff softly smiled, stepped past and slapped the old man lightly upon the shoulders, then he walked back out into roadway sunlight. It was high noon. He briefly wondered where the morning had gone and struck out for the cafe. He was not especially hungry but he could always eat a piece of pie, even if it was greasy. He also wanted to sit somewhere for a few minutes and sort out some thoughts.

When Sam returned to town he was going to be fighting mad. He was also going to arrive at about the same conclusion which had motivated Frank Morgan to ride to town this morning, and Cliff decided he did not want to be around. Not at least until Sam had talked to Morgan.

The cafeman was having a cup of coffee and working his teeth with a toothpick. He got Cliff the pie, watched him start on it, then said, "I've noticed over the years that when a man's been widdered or his wife's run off or something, the first thing he misses is sweets. Like that pie."

Cliff looked up. "Did you ever try to cook anything without floating it in grease, Will?"

The cafeman went right on picking his teeth and sipping black java. "Yeah, once, and everything burnt all to hell. . . . Where's Sam this morning? I thought I seen him ride out with some fellers from town."

"He's gone lookin' for the tooth fairy."

Will tossed away the toothpick and put a stern gaze upon his only customer. "You're in a clever mood this morning, ain't you? Want some coffee to wash away the grease?"

Cliff finished the pie as Barney Sandal walked in looking gray and wet-eyed. He called for black coffee and sank dispiritedly down at the counter beside Cliff. "What a hell of a night," he moaned. "And this morning too." He looked over. "Is that pie greasy?"

"Yeah."

"Then I'd better stick to black coffee . . . Did you hear that friend of yours, Gutierrez, was going to get married?"

"Yeah. He told me."

"Well; I got an old bottle of champagne I been keeping until someone came along who knew what it was. I figure to send that over."

Cliff smiled. Champagne—hell, everyone knew what it was—and they'd pay a big price for a bottle of it. Especially an old bottle of it. He arose, dropped some coins on the counter and gave Barney one of those friendly light slaps on the shoulder too. Some men just could not admit they had ever been wrong, but if they had consciences they would find some way of *showing* it.

"He'll appreciate that, Barney."

Sandal groaned and reached with both hands when the cafeman arrived with the mug of black coffee.

Outside, Cliff decided to avoid his house for a while and strolled on up to the gunshop where there were usually some loafers telling lies about their marksmanship. From up there, he could keep an eye on the roadway and see Sam when the posse returned.

FOURTEEN
"Just Wait!"

The four men with Sam Hart looked disgruntled when they trooped back down Main Street behind the sheriff, and they did not even go down as far as the jailhouse with him, they split off, two heading for home, the other two walking their mounts towards Saul Hanson's barn.

Sam stamped off dust and stalked into the jailhouse. Cliff watched it all from the gunshop window and as soon as the door closed behind his brother-in-law, he struck out for the lower end of town.

Only one of those possemen was still down there. A lanky, rawboned red-headed man who assisted at the blacksmith shop, and was bitterly complaining to an interested Saul Hanson that they had wasted the whole darned day riding out to the Morgan place and riding back again.

"Not a soul was there but a Chinese cook and a Messican who wrangles the horses. Even Jess warn't there. And Mister Morgan was gone too. And you aren't goin' to believe this, Saul, but all Morgan's riders quit last night and slipped out in the night. One of 'em left a note. The cook told us that. One of them cowboys left this note sayin' they didn't figure to hang around if the law was on its way. That's all it said. Just that they wasn't goin' to be around if a posse come . . . And Sam was so mad I thought he'd explode. All the way back he was cussing someone for warning those men out there. I've never see him so mad."

Saul sympathetically waggled his head. After the posseman walked away beating dust from his trouser-legs with a disreputable hat, Saul said, "You hear that, Cliff?"

Anyone could have heard it, even if they'd been up by the cottonwood trees out front. Cliff nodded.

Saul pursed his lips for a moment in thought before speaking again. "Who could have warned them boys? Someone from town, maybe early this morning?"

"Saul, that feller said they was warned last night, not this morning; that they rode out last night."

Hanson reconsidered. "But who would have known a posse was coming last night?"

Cliff's answer was cryptic. "Did you ever try to keep a secret in Morgan Valley?"

Hanson gave up. "Come on down to the harness-room with me."

Cliff went. It was getting along towards afternoon so maybe whiskied coffee wouldn't be too terrible. In the morning, the way Saul Hanson usually started his day with laced coffee, though, was not just too early, it was also unappetizing.

But Cliff did not get a chance to sample the liveryman's concoction. His brother-in-law appeared in the runway. One of the hostlers came up from out back. Cliff heard the sheriff say, "Where does Cliff Stanton keep his animal?"

Cliff held up a hand when Saul would have gone out there. They heard Sam Hart walking away, spurs ringing, as the dayman led off. Cliff turned to Saul, "Who took a horse out last night?" He had a failing heart as he asked, because he knew who it had to be. But Hanson's answer was brief.

"No one. I collect from the nighthawk every mornin' when I come to work. He didn't rent out a single beast last night."

Cliff stared, then turned as his brother-in-law came back up through. Either Lew had got that horse he'd ridden elsewhere—or the nighthawk was knocking-down on Saul. Either way was fine with Cliff.

He stepped out and faced the sheriff. "How did you make out?" he asked, and Sam stopped in his tracks, glared, then, seeing the dayman and Hanson both looking, he jerked his head. "Come on out front, Cliff."

Sam was still angry but the cold fury had died out

some time earlier. He had one of those tempers which exploded into white-hot fury in one moment, then burned itself out over the next twenty seconds and became just solid anger. When he turned, up by the old cottonwood tree, he said, "I don't know how you did it, but sure as hell—"

"I did not do it, Sam. Right after you left last night I went to bed and didn't leave that bed until this morning. Did you talk to Frank Morgan?"

"Yeah. What of it?"

"Did he say he thought I rode out there last night?"

"He said he was plumb convinced you *didn't* ride out there. And that's another thing: He refused to say why. But he told me he was ready to post bail if I wanted to arrest him, then he was going over to Denver and bring back the fightingest lawyer they got over there. And— if he's acquitted he said he's goin' to sue me and the town for a whole passle of things, starting with false arrest and finishing up with something like character smirchin' which I never ran into before . . . Cliff; who else knew I was going out there?"

"Who else did you tell, Sam? Seems to me you told me without any encouragement. Who else did you shoot your mouth off to?"

"I didn't *shoot my mouth off!*"

"Sam; you didn't just tell me, I'll bet money on that. Maybe you didn't have to tell folks anyway. Maybe those rangeriders had one smart one among them and he scairt out the rest of them."

"Maybe this, maybe that," retorted the sheriff. "I got

132

enough maybes now to fill a cellar. I got them all the way back to town from those nitwits I taken with me. Cliff . . . to my dyin' day I'm going to believe you had *something* to do with it. I know you. I know how you think about that kind of a hanging. I just wish I knew for a plumb fact you were in it. I'd rattle your darned cage for you!"

Cliff turned emphatic. "Sam, folks won't lose respect for you. You did what you thought had to be done."

The vein up alongside Sheriff Hart's temple swelled and throbbed. "Save your damned sermons for Sunday," he growled. "You know what's happened now, don't you? You and those In'ian trackers are all the witnesses."

Cliff was shaking his head before his brother-in-law had finished speaking. "I'm no witness. I didn't see anyone get hung. I didn't see anyone catch a pair of rustlers or even come close to them."

"But you sent Frank Morgan in that direction and you figured those boys was rustlers. Don't deny that because you told me that yourself."

"Sam—damn it—all I told you was that I'd met Frank Morgan out there and told him where I'd seen a little drive of cattle. That's all I did. And now by golly I think I'll catch the evening coach for Denver and spend a few weeks over there."

Sheriff Hart loosened his stance a little, hooked both thumbs and regarded his brother-in-law. "You don't have to go to Denver. The circuit-rider was in town off the morning stage when I got back. He's got a room up at the boarding-house." Sam sighed. "I talked an hour with him. He won't let me do it."

"Do what?"

"Hold a trial for Morgan. 'Insufficient evidence' he calls it. I got to put together a better case, and maybe next month when he rides through again he'll hear the case."

Cliff was pleased. "Did you tell Morgan that when he was at your office?"

"How did you know he was over there?"

"Well, damn it, I got eyes haven't I?"

"Well. At least I told him he hadn't scairt *all* my witnesses off. Well, that *some*one had not scairt them all off. I told him about you and the In'ians."

Cliff looked disbelieving. "You're out to nail Frank Morgan, yet you told him who the witnesses against him would be? Sam, by tomorrow morning there won't be a single bronco anywhere around Centreville. You spilled the beans to the one man around Morgan Valley who can just keep droppin' gold coins into their hats until they sell you out and ride away."

Sheriff Hart, for some reason, did not look mortified, if in fact he felt that way. He said, "I'm getting old, Cliff. It's not even sundown yet and I'm tired to the bone." Sam was garrulous now, and if his anger was still simmering it no longer showed, not even when he said, "I'll treat you to supper at the cafe tonight. Do you good."

Someone came along to tell Sam his prisoners were raising hell at the jailhouse. Sam shrugged and picked up his hat. "Let's go eat. What I really need is a slug of whisky."

They did not go directly to the cafe. Instead, they bellied up to Barney Sandal's bar. Barney was not there. His barman said he'd been in briefly then had gone back home. The barman impishly grinned over this.

They leaned in the nearly empty big old dingy room which never ceased smelling of man-sweat, tobacco-smoke, horse-sweat and spilled liquor, which in fact was a pleasant, relaxing aroma in the one area of town where only men could relax, had a bottle and two glasses before them atop the bar, and as Sheriff Hart began to feel a little less like a rag doll he thoughtfully said, "I don't want to give up. It's not in my nature. Especially with a son of a bitch like Frank Morgan who already thinks he's gawd on horseback."

Cliff stirred his whisky by turning the little sticky glass forth and back between his palms. "Right now you remind me of an army officer I knew once. He was brave and all. He always did his duty, and usually he did it real well, Sam—in a lousy cause."

Hart was not irritated. "Murder isn't a lousy cause, Cliff."

"Tryin' to nail someone's hide to the fence over something half, maybe even two-thirds of the people believe is right, *is* a lousy cause, Sam."

"The law says—"

"Sam, damn it all, those books of law you read were made by folks who never saw the frontier, let alone lived on it. Sure, it's tidy to have laws you can look up and comply with, because then you don't have to think for yourself. Some gunsel back in New York or Massachusetts already thought it all out for you—and he didn't know his rear-end from a round rock about what things are like out here."

Sam refilled his glass. He was one of those men who truly enjoyed the taste of whisky. He sipped it, gazed at his leathery, bronzed features in the back-bar mirror and sipped some more of it.

Someone came in from the roadway. It was wiry little Amos Shepler from the stage company's corralyard. He walked up beside Cliff, beaming as he waved the barman away. Amos was a teetotaller; maybe that was what made him so high-strung and unpredictable. He said, "Cliff, you'll be pleased to know the regular whip for the night run is going to take it south tonight."

Cliff was indeed pleased, mainly because he had forgot all about his promise. He nodded to Shepler. "Glad to hear he's up and around. Like I told you, Amos, I don't want to get back into that business. Care for a drink?"

Shepler wrinkled his nose, shook his head and turned to depart. Cliff watched from the back-bar mirror. Shepler even sort of loped along like a rabbit. Cliff put the man out of his mind as his brother-in-law spoke as he lifted his hat to scratch.

"I sent in letters for the bounty on those two hanged fellers, but I sure don't want to see Morgan get it. Even if he needed it I'd hate to see him get it."

136

"Then why did you put in for it? He's sure the one deserves it, if he hung those men."

"What the hell do you mean—if? You know blamed well he hung 'em."

Cliff reached to refill his little glass. He did not reply; along that route lay only a renewal of their old argument. As far as he was concerned he was tired of the entire affair. He dropped the whisky straight down and blinked at the quick rush of tears.

Two dusty rangemen strode in beating off dust with their hats. They were strangers to Cliff, and when Sam took an interest, as he always did with newcomers to Morgan Valley, one of them said they had just been hired to ride for a man named Morgan, who was down at the liverybarn at the same time they had been putting up their horses. They grinned. It was the quickest they had ever found work in their lives.

"Just barely got into town and there's this stocky feller with the silver horn-cap and breedy horse waitin' to hire us on."

Cliff watched his brother-in-law's face. Sam studied the strangers with a slightly vinegary expression, then he said, "He's the biggest cowman around here. He's a good man to work for. I never rode for him but I've known a lot of fellers who have. They always said he was a fair man, paid well, and never asked more'n riders was ready to do anyway."

Cliff looked into his little empty glass. Sam turned as though to defend himself and said to his brother-in-law, "Well, you even give the devil his due, don't you?"

Cliff laughed.

They returned to the late-day roadway. Centreville was quiet, dusk was on its way, the road was nearly empty; it was that between-time of day; folks were at home, or maybe at the boarding-house, but anyway they were washing up for supper, merchants were tidying up their shelves, tallying up their money for the day and preparing to close down for the night.

Frank Morgan walked his handsome chestnut gelding up the center of the roadway from Hanson's barn, the only person riding through. He saw Cliff and the sheriff and angled towards their side of the roadway. Where he stopped, just beyond the gnawed old hitch-rail in front of Barney's saloon, and rested both gloved hands atop the saddlehorn, he gazed unwaveringly at the sheriff.

"About those two men someone hanged," he said, and Sam Hart snorted, which Morgan ignored as he went on speaking. "I was just talking to Hanson at the liverybarn. He's president of the school board, he told me, and they've got difficulties. Sheriff, if there are rewards for those two rustlers, do you think it would be a good idea to turn that money over to the school district?"

Cliff had never heard Frank Morgan solicit an opinion from anyone else before, but then he didn't really know Morgan that well, either. He knew his *type* though, and they did not ask for opinions.

Sam seemed equally as surprised, which may have been why he stood there returning the cowman's gaze for so long before answering.

"I think it would be a good idea, Mister Morgan. I heard last winter they was in financial trouble. And I already wrote about that reward-money. There wouldn't be anyone else to give it to anyway, as far as I can see."

Frank Morgan studied Sam Hart for an additional few moments. "Sheriff, one thing you told me today is true. Times change and folks have to change with them."

Sam solemnly said, "Mind putting that into words that make sense to me, Mister Morgan?"

"Hanging them on the spot is the quickest way, but maybe not the best way, any more. Men like that just aren't worth risking prison over. That's what I meant."

Cliff was hoping Sam would not start an argument. What Morgan had just admitted was that he may have been hasty in his anger; that if this ever happened again, he would profit from what he had learned this time and leave punishment to book-law.

Sam picked words before answering the cowman. "Well; I expect if things wasn't going to change from how they used to be, Mister Morgan, I wouldn't be standin' here wearin' this badge. I'll take it kindly, havin' your support from now on."

Morgan showed a vestige of thin smile then switched his attention towards Cliff. "I owe you an apology," he said, and because this sort of thing always embarrassed Cliff, he made a swift reply.

"Naw; it wasn't me, like I told you, but whoever it was—he did the right thing."

After Morgan had ridden slowly on up through town Sam turned. "It *had* to be you, damn it all."

Cliff sighed. "It wasn't, Sam."

"All right, then who was it rode out there and spooked those riders, tell me that!"

Cliff smiled. "I wouldn't tell you that if you agreed to buy my supper at the cafe for the next six months."

"But you know, darn your hide."

Cliff turned to lead off in the direction of the cafe. "Someday I'll tell you. Maybe in the next four or five years when we're standin' together out at the cemetery. Sure I know who it was."

"You are withholding evidence, Cliff."

They looked at one another. "Sam; tell me something straight out. Back yonder when we were talkin' and I said Morgan could drop money into the hats of those warwhoop-trackers of yours and get them to disappear, you didn't act upset at all."

"What of it?"

"You should have reacted differently, Sam, *if* you believe all that crap you been spoutin' about the law."

Sheriff Hart sighed and looked down towards the southern end of town when he answered. "What I been tellin' you, is that it's my *duty;* that I get paid for upholdin' the law. I never once told you I always agreed with the law and I never said I sympathize with it. All I said was that I got my job to do. As for what Morgan did—hangin' bastards like that is the best way to handle them, whether he or the law does it." Sam halted to hold the cafe door for his brother-in-law to enter first. "The thing is, Cliff, if I can't make a decent case against Morgan, why then I just plain can't. But I got to try, you see? If he beats me out somehow, well at least I tried, didn't I, and that clears my conscience."

They went over to straddle the counter-bench. They were the first customers for supper because it was a little early. The cafeman came along wiping both palms on his shirt-front and chewing on a wooden toothpick. He hadn't shaved since the day before, and since freezing his feet on a trail-drive seven years earlier he had never felt comfortable in anything but a loose pair of old carpet slippers.

"Hog jowls with black-eyed peas," he announced, "and fresh coffee and no pie tonight but I got some watery custard."

They nodded. After Will had padded away to his cooking area they looked after him. Cliff sighed. Nothing had changed after all. "Someday a woman'll come to town and open a decent beanery, Sam, then we won't have to scrape bear grease off the top of our mouths after eatin' here."

Sheriff Hart had never been married so he was more philosophical about what circumstances had reduced him to eating. "I got to take two trays across the road to the Sloats," he said, ignoring his brother-in-law's uncharitable implication. "And if you think this grub is bad—where the hell *did* you get that beef we ate last night?"

Cliff remembered something. "You know old man Sanchez?"

"Feller who used to work for Lew Calkins? Yeah, what about him?"

"Al Gutierrez is going to marry his daughter."

"By golly she's pretty enough for *any*one to want to marry, for a damned fact."

"Sanchez made some fresh *chorriz* and Al brought me up some of it this morning."

Sheriff Hart looked pained. "You're not going to eat it are you? One time someone gave me some of that stuff and I put it out back for the dogs. You know what? Not a darned one of those dogs would touch it."

"What I was trying to say, Sam, was that I'll rassle it up for breakfast in the morning if you'd care to—"

"I wouldn't eat that damned stuff if I had nothing else to eat for a year. Cliff, you got to get a housekeeper, or maybe at least a lady to come in once in a while and cook you some decent grub."

The cafeman shuffled along with their platters, and as he went to fill coffee cups too, he said, "You fellers heard that Barney's sick."

They hadn't heard it but it did not surprise them.

"He taken the night stage for Preston to see the doctor down there."

Sam Hart dryly responded to this scrap of information. "By now he'd ought to be smart enough never to drink his own whisky. Only to sell it for other folks to drink. Will, how come that custard's so watery?"

"I told you it was watered, Sheriff. I didn't have enough of the stuff you make it out of so I sort of watered it a little." Having disposed of this topic in a

142

perfectly normal way the cafeman also said, "Miz Hamm's sister's comin' out to stay a spell with her—her being widowed and all. You ever see her sister? She was out here three, four years ago. She's a schoolma'm back somewhere in Kansas. I figure she's about the prettiest woman I ever seen, and I've looked at a lot of them all the way from Nebraska to Texas to up here."

Sam was not particularly interested. "She married, Will?"

"Nope. She's a widow too. Strange you fellers didn't see her last time she come visiting. She's sure a pretty lady. Little; not much bigger'n colt, lean and hung together just exactly right. Got green eyes and the prettiest mouth you ever saw, for a fact. Got a funny name, I can't recall right now. Martin told me one time it was an Irish name."

Cliff raised his eyes. "You remember all that after four years?"

Will rolled his eyes. "Wait. Just you boys wait until you see her. You'll know why I remembered her . . . You want more coffee?"

Sam looked into his cup. It was empty and he did not even remember drinking the contents. As Will turned away Sam nudged Cliff. "There's your answer, like a miracle. Little and neat and pretty."

Cliff looked over. "Are you crazy? I haven't even seen this woman. Anyway, I don't want to get—"

"Like Will just told you, wait. Just you wait, Cliff."

Cliff said, "Oh hell," in a tone of disgust and went back to his meal.

Center Point Publishing
600 Brooks Road ● PO Box 1
Thorndike ME 04986-0001 USA

(207) 568-3717

US & Canada:
1 800 929-9108
www.centerpointlargeprint.com